I0685551

PATHS
OF
DESTINY

THE DESTINY TRILOGY (BOOK 2)

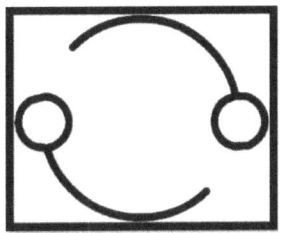

PATHS
OF
DESTINY

THE DESTINY TRILOGY (BOOK 2)

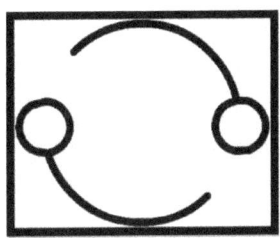

Cris Pasqueralle

Cosby Media Productions
Entertaining the Mind, and Tempting the Soul

Paths of Destiny: Book 2 of The Destiny Trilogy

Copyright © 2015 by Cris Pasqueralle. All rights reserved.
No part of this publication may be reproduced, stored in a retrieval
system or transmitted in any way by any means, electronic, mechanical,
photocopy, recording or otherwise without the prior permission of the
author except as provided by USA copyright law.
The opinions expressed by the author are not necessarily those of Cosby
Media Productions.
Published by Cosby Media Productions.
www.cosbymediaproductions.com
Cover art: Cosby Media Productions
Editor: Tamar Hela
ISBN-13: 978-0692582107
ISBN-10: 069258210X

Dedication

Paths of Destiny is dedicated to the two people who helped make this story the best it can be: My editors, Tamar Hela and Toniann Pasqueralle.

Thanks for everything.

TABLE OF CONTENTS

Maddie

The sun slowly rose over the mountains, Tardon and his followers had vanished from the battle scene, and Jack was lying on the ground. Tina was unconscious, buried in a pile of rubble and, most likely, badly injured. Ray ran to Tina, while Connie took care of Jack. She knelt beside him and assessed the bumps and bruises on his face. He was groggy, but managed to smile at Connie before falling unconscious.

Benny surveyed the scene and called out to anyone within earshot. "Has anyone seen Maddie?" He waited for a reply, but none came.

He then found his way to Stanton, who was walking through the grounds of Tardon's nearly destroyed village, taking inventory of his fighting force. Some lay on the ground with various injuries; others merely rested from the battle awaiting orders.

"Stanton," Benny called.

The figure dressed in white stopped and turned. The breeze blew his mane of red hair and beard about his face. He waited for Benny to catch up.

"We need to find Maddie," Benny said.

Stanton was calm. "Yes, now that Tardon has had a taste of their power, we must keep the twins together."

Benny sighed. "Agreed, but I haven't seen her."

Stanton looked at Benny for a moment and then beckoned to the crowd. "Members of the guard, we must find the young girl called Maddie. Has anyone seen her?"

One of the Mountain Gnomes stepped forward. His clothes were torn, his face was covered with bruises, and his shirt was bloodstained. He cleared his throat before speaking. "Sir, the girl-wizard and the lady—they vanished at the start of the battle."

"This is my fault," Benny whispered. "I knew Lisa didn't belong here. I should have insisted that she stay behind." He turned to Stanton. "We must search for them."

Stanton put a hand on Benny's shoulder. "Breathe, my friend. Of course we will search for them, but we cannot allow Tardon to know the twins have been separated." He closed his eyes for several seconds, and when he opened them, Gavin and Connie were walking towards him.

"You called?" Gavin said, as they approached.

Stanton looked them over. They both carried signs of the battle, but did not appear to be seriously injured. "How is Jack?" he asked Connie.

"I don't think he has any serious physical injuries," she replied. "But he is emotionally drained; I'm sure he'll be fine after some rest, though."

"That is good news," Stanton said. "However, we do have a problem. Maddie and Lisa are missing, and I don't need to tell you how important it is for us to find them."

Benny coughed.

"Very well, Benjamin," Stanton acknowledged. "How important it is for us to find *Maddie*." He turned to Gavin. "Since you know Lisa better than most, I want you to take Connie and go to all the places you think Lisa would take Maddie. Keep us well informed."

Gavin wasted no time; he took Connie's hand and vanished.

"Benny," Stanton said. "Take Tina, Ray, and Jack back to your home. I will meet you there shortly."

While Benny went to gather his friends, Stanton addressed the members of his guard. "My brave and loyal guard: you have done extremely well here today. Return to your homes and rest. I will be in contact before long. Thank you for your efforts."

One by one, the members of the guard began to vanish. As Stanton watched, Togo walked up to him. "May I be of any service to you?" he asked.

"I believe we've asked enough from you for now," Stanton said. "I wish to thank you and your fellow Gnomes. Your bravery has no boundaries." He put a hand on Togo's shoulder. "Go home, my friend. We will talk soon."

Togo bowed and returned to the other Gnomes.

Stanton looked around the village and sighed. "What are you up to, Lisa?" he said to himself. Then he closed his eyes and vanished.

Maddie

Maddie and Lisa appeared out of nothing and arrived in a small living room. The walls were off-white, the floor was dark wood with a large circular area rug in the center, a glass-topped coffee table sat in the middle of the rug, and along its edges were a couch, love seat, and two armchairs. Lisa took her arm off of Maddie and left the room.

Maddie simply stood there, her chest heaving and large tears flowing down her face. Her whole body shook, and she chewed her bottom lip and kept looking around as if she expected someone to show up and tell her it was all a bad dream. Within a few seconds, Lisa returned, carrying a cup that held steaming liquid. She handed the cup to Maddie, and a few drops spilled over the side as she took it in her trembling hands.

"Oh, sweetheart," Lisa said, as she put an arm around Maddie and guided her to a chair. "Please, sit down so I can try to explain things." She eased Maddie into an armchair and sat in the one next to her. "Drink," she urged, gesturing to the cup in Maddie's hands.

Maddie looked at the clear, hot liquid and took a small sip. Then she breathed deeply, attempting to gain some sort of composure. "I need to get back to my family," she said.

Lisa looked down her nose and shook her head, her black hair swaying back and forth. "Right now, you need to stay out of harm's way."

Maddie took another sip from the cup. "My whole family is in harm's way *right now*, and I have no idea what's happening to them. I need to get back to the fight."

Lisa leaned forward and put her hand on top of Maddie's knee. "Sweetheart, I know how you feel. Your parents and brother are my family too, but Stanton and his guard are on the scene, and I trust his abilities, as well as those of your parents. You are destined for great things, and I won't take the risk that something might happen to you."

Maddie took another sip from her cup. "What great things are you talking about?!"

Lisa leaned back and crossed her legs. "You are destined to lead the magical realm to its rightful place as the first realm."

"What are you talking about?" Maddie repeated.

"You have been chosen for a great task," her aunt calmly replied. "You will unite the realms under a magical rule and save them from destruction."

Maddie sat back and scratched her head. "No, the realms can't mix; magic can't rule over the realms. Uncle Benny said so."

"They can," Lisa contradicted. "And you will be the one to do it."

Maddie closed her eyes for a moment, trying to process what Lisa was saying. "I don't understand any of this," she said, pulling her legs close to her chest, wrapping her arms around them, and slowly beginning to rock back and forth. "I want my mother."

"I can explain all of this when you are bit more calm." Lisa got up from the chair. "I'll send a message to your parents and let them know you're safe." Then she left the room.

Maddie looked at the cup she was holding. The warm liquid had a minty flavor and seemed to soothe and relax her. She took another sip, put the cup on the coffee table, and then leaned back in the chair and closed her eyes.

Lisa came back to the room and saw that Maddie had fallen asleep. She waved a hand and Maddie was lifted into the air and laid gently on the couch. A second wave of Lisa's hand placed a blanket over her niece.

"Rest well," Lisa said. "Tomorrow, I will lead you to your true destiny."

Jack

It was just before dawn, and a dark figure crouched behind a garbage dumpster in a store parking lot. The mist clung to him like the smell of the rotting food clinging to the dumpster. A delivery van pulled up to the back door of a deli, and Jack Austin knew he'd be able to get away from the foul odor in just a few minutes.

The driver got out of the van, piled three large boxes on the concrete steps, and was gone. Jack waited another thirty seconds before running to the boxes. He grabbed two-foot long hero breads from one box, three rolls from another, and two bagels from the last. As he dashed off, he heard the metal clank of the deli's back door being opened and knew that he'd just beaten the clerk again.

Jack walked around the side of the row of stores and saw a meat delivery truck parked at the front of the deli and smiled; a two-for-one was rare. He watched as the driver got out and opened the refrigerated back of the truck. The man piled several large boxes onto a cart and wheeled them into the deli. Jack knew it would take a while to unload the cart, so he ran to the truck. He jumped into the back and quickly located a small turkey breast. Holding it under his arm like a football, he turned to leave the truck, but froze mid-step. A very large and angry man blocked the exit.

"What the hell are you doing?!" the man yelled.

Jack shook off the initial shock of being caught and looked the man in the eyes. He spoke calmly. "I'm just getting something to eat, that's all." Then he waved a hand, and the man stepped aside and smiled.

"Have a nice day, sir," the man said.

Jack jumped from the back of the truck and walked away. It was unusual for him to use magic; he actually hated it and everything associated with it, but he also wasn't about to be caught stealing. He knew it was wrong, but he needed to fend for himself and viewed it as a kind of modern day hunting. There was a time when people hunted and gathered just to stay alive; they foraged the woods and meadows for food, eating whatever they could find. Well, where Jack lived, there were no woods and meadows in which to hunt and gather, so he hunted and gathered what his surroundings provided.

Jack stayed close to the fence line as he made his way back to the house he had once shared with his family. The neighborhood had woken up, and lights were on in nearly every home as people readied themselves for the day. Jack climbed through the basement window he'd left propped open, locked it behind him, and headed to the kitchen.

It had been a couple of months since he had left his family in the magical realm to return to his life in the non-magical world, but it wasn't a return to the normal teenage life he had once enjoyed. He was alone, though he didn't think that would last long. He felt certain that as soon as his mother, Tina, recovered from her injuries, she would come for him. However, that hadn't happened yet. Jack figured it was because his parents were preoccupied with locating his sister.

Maddie had disappeared with their Aunt Lisa during the battle with Tardon and his followers, and Jack had heard nothing of her whereabouts. He missed Maddie; they were twins, and their connection was strong—at least, Jack had once believed that it was. Now, he wasn't so sure. Maybe his family was doing better without him. Maybe Maddie had been right all along, and his family wanted to stay in the magical realm, even if their son wasn't with them. Jack shook his head. That couldn't be true; something else had to be going on.

He had drawn all the shades in the house so any passersby wouldn't see him through the windows. From what he'd learned since his return, everyone thought something terrible had happened to the Austin family, and a major search for them had taken place. It made sense to Jack. After all, he and Maddie hadn't been to school in weeks, and their parents hadn't been to work. Someone must have missed them and reported their disappearance. That was why Jack had found crime scene tape surrounding the house and discarded rubber gloves strewn about in every room. He guessed that, to the authorities, it must have looked like something terrible had happened—which it had.

The attack Tardon launched in the Austin home left damage and more than a few signs of a struggle. With birthday decorations still up and a half-eaten cake rotting in the kitchen, it didn't appear that the Austins had gone on vacation. The broken coffee table and the damage to one of the walls pointed the investigators to something more sinister, but from what Jack had heard, the investigation had hit a wall and was at a standstill.

Jack walked past all the reminders of the battle on his way to the kitchen. Once there, he took out a knife, the rolls, and the turkey, and made himself a large sandwich. The electricity had been turned off, as had the phone and the heat. It seemed that even if a person was the victim of some terrible crime, the bills still needed to be paid. The water still worked, but it was cold, and Jack had learned to take very fast showers. However, he knew the water would eventually be turned off as well.

Several bank notices were also sent to the house, and one of them posted on the door stated that the owners were no longer current on their mortgage and the property would be subject to auction. Jack had done some research into foreclosure at the library and figured he still had a few months of living there before the bank came to empty the house and get it ready to sell. However, he knew he'd have to leave eventually; someone had to find his sister.

Jack

After eating breakfast, Jack carefully wrapped the uncut portion of the turkey in a plastic bag and brought it to the basement. This was where he'd set up living quarters. Since he'd learned that people around here believed him and his family to be missing, he thought it best not to be seen. He'd moved his mattress and several blankets to a corner of the basement and set up several large boxes around it so that if anyone did happen to go inside the house and find their way downstairs, it would look like just another pile of old junk. He'd also covered over the basement windows with dark-colored towels so no one could look in. It was a good thing he had.

School had let out for the summer a couple of weeks ago, and the neighborhood kids—some of them Jack and Maddie's old friends—came snooping around every few days. Jack could hear them in the yard, all giving their own versions of why and how the Austin family disappeared. One of the kids thought that Mr. Austin was a member of the mafia and he'd crossed the wrong person. Another thought that they'd all been abducted by aliens. And one was close to the truth when he said he thought the whole family were spies who'd been called back to their country. *If they only knew.*

Jack put the turkey in a cooler he'd found in the basement that he resupplied with ice every couple of days from the machine at the local volunteer firehouse, which was seldom locked.

At the right time of night, Jack would sneak in, grab some ice and the occasional soda, and get out without being noticed. Since he still had a few hours before he could carry out his planned activity for the day, he decided to get some sleep. He found it easiest to sleep during the day because the quiet of the night brought back memories of his recent battles and a longing for the life he had with his family before he knew he was a wizard. He lay on the mattress, moved a few boxes around to better conceal himself, and closed his eyes.

Jack was awakened by the sound of a woman calling his name. It was very faint, but he was sure he'd heard it. He knew the voice: it was his mother. Jack leapt from his fortress and ran up the stairs, his heart racing. She'd finally come back for him. He knew she would.

He called out. "Mom! Where are you?"

But there was no answer. Jack tore through the house, searching every room, yet no one was there. He sat at the top of the stairs and hung his head. It must have been a dream.

Dejected, Jack went back to the basement and grabbed a backpack where he had some notebooks, pens, and his mother's laptop. He put on a hooded sweatshirt, tying the hood tight around his head. In the summer heat, he would look odd wearing this, but at least no one would recognize him.

After making sure no one was around, he climbed out the basement window, left it opened just a crack, and headed for what had become his sanctuary. The one place he knew that none of his friends would be during the summer: the public library.

Once in the library, Jack found a spot in the far back of the building, behind the numerous rows of books, in a study cubicle. The sides were high, and it was made for only one person, so no one would join him. Not that he had to worry much about that. But for a few old men reading magazines, and the occasional toddler story time group, no one was ever here.

There was an electrical outlet under the table that Jack used to recharge the battery on the laptop. Once it was plugged in, he went about finding the books he'd read the previous day. Jack truly wanted nothing to do with the magical realm. The people there had done nothing but lie to him—even his family. But he missed his sister, and, as far as he knew, she still hadn't been found after disappearing during their parents' rescue. Something told him that if he ever wanted to see Maddie again, he'd have to find her himself. So, if he did have to go back, Jack would be prepared.

Since his return, Jack had read everything he could about wizards. The myths, the stories, even accounts of people who claimed to be wizards or to have been in contact with them. He read about Wicca and witches' covens, stories of Merlin the Great, as well as the stories of King Solomon and his supposed magical powers that were never taught in Sunday school. All of it seemed to be based on people's imaginations and not very likely to help Jack in his quest for magical knowledge. Still, it was interesting reading, and it kept his days occupied.

Today, Jack read through a how-to manual on becoming a wizard. It spoke about wizardry as a religion and how a person had to commit themselves to the elements of the earth to get in touch with their true selves; only then could the wizard inside all of us be let out. Jack laughed. He knew that wizards were *born*, not *made*, and there certainly wasn't a wizard inside of everyone.

He went through the book, and even made notes on types of herbs that could be used to heal wounds and sicknesses. This was something, which, if true, could come in handy.

When he finished gathering what might be useful, Jack turned to his laptop and typed in the word "wizards," and then scrolled through the numerous websites that popped up. Something caught his eye. A website for a man called "The Hawk." "See The Hawk in action," it read. "This modern day Merlin performs feats and illusions that are mind blowing." Now *this*, Jack had to see.

Maddie

Maddie opened her eyes and found that she was lying on the couch in her aunt's living room. She sat up and gasped. Sitting across from her was a girl not much older than she was. The girl had long blonde hair and was dressed in red—the same red that Maddie had seen the Tars wear. Maddie leapt up and raised her hand.

"Maddie!" Lisa yelled as she entered the room. "That's no way to treat a guest." She placed a tray of pastries on the coffee table and sat in the chair opposite the newcomer.

Maddie looked from Lisa, to the girl, and back to Lisa. "But she's wearing Tardon's colors. I thought he sent her for me."

Lisa smiled. "Maddie, you must know that things are not always as they appear. Yes, Erin here does wear the colors of the Tars, and she is a Tar, but you cannot assume that she means you harm. None of the Tars mean you harm."

Maddie sat down again. "How can you say that? They kidnapped my parents, they captured my brother and Benny, they—"

"They didn't hurt you, did they?" Lisa asked.

Maddie leaned back. "No, but they did—"

It was the girl who interrupted this time. "They did nothing harmful unless they were provoked."

Maddie looked at Lisa again, and then at the girl. "Who are you?" she said.

"I'm sorry; I didn't mean to be rude. My name is Erin and I am Lisa's student."

"Student?" Maddie questioned.

"Yes," Lisa replied. "Did you think Benny was the only one who could teach the wizarding way?"

Maddie scratched her head. "Umm, yeah, I kind of did."

Lisa and Erin both laughed, and then Erin spoke. "Benny only teaches those who he wants to push his and Stanton's views on. He will never tell you the truth of the differences that divide the magical realm."

"But he *has* told me," Maddie countered.

"I can guess what he's told you," Erin said. "He told you that Tardon wishes to mix the realms of existence, that this mixture will cause instability throughout the world, and that, eventually, the instability will cause the world's destruction. Sound familiar?"

"Yes," Maddie answered. "He did tell me that, but it makes a lot of sense."

"Does it?" Erin continued. "Does it make sense that someone would want to put in place a system of checks and balances to destroy themselves? Tardon and the Tars only wish to place magic at the forefront of the realms, that's all."

Maddie shook her head. "No, Tardon is evil; I've seen it."

"Have you?" Erin prompted. "What have you seen?"

"He kidnapped my parents!"

"In order to get you to the magical realm, if he came to you, do you think for one second that Benny would have allowed him to state his case and tell you of your destiny?"

"But he attacked us," Maddie insisted. "He sent the Thunderbird after me and Jack." She thought about how she and Jack had defeated the large bird, and how Stanton had told them it was because of their concern for one another. Recalling the memory made her realize that she missed her brother very much.

"I've been told this happened during your training. Are you sure it wasn't one of Benny's lessons?" Erin asked.

Maddie shook her head. "No, Benny was very upset about it; he didn't do it."

Erin shrugged. "Perhaps."

"What about the attack on the Gnomes' forest? Tardon sent those animals against the Gnomes," Maddie retorted.

Erin had an answer ready. "The Gnomes have kept the animals of the forest under their control for centuries; sooner or later, they were going to rise up against them. You and your brother just happened to be here when they did."

Maddie shook her head again. "No, that's not right."

Erin sat beside Maddie on the couch and took her hand. "There are a lot of things that aren't right, but you can fix them all. You are the destined one; you are the one destined to rule over the realms, to put them in their proper balance, so that the harmony of the world will be restored."

Maddie leaned back and held her head in her hands.

Lisa stood. "This is a lot for you to take in. Eat something; gather your thoughts, and then anything you ask, we will answer." She motioned for Erin to follow her, and they went into the kitchen, leaving Maddie to ponder all she had heard.

Lisa and Erin sat at the kitchen table, and Lisa smiled. "You've done very well," she said.

Erin bowed her head. "Thank you, but I believe we have more work to do with this one."

Maddie

Maddie sat on the couch, nibbling on a pastry and thinking about what she'd just heard. Jack had always thought that Benny wasn't telling them the whole truth, but could this be what he didn't want them to know? Was Tardon's view of things correct? No, it couldn't be. Why would her parents have fought against Tardon if he was right? Did Benny lie to them too? Were her parents denied the truth as well? Was Maddie really destined to rule over a magical realm that ruled all of existence? She'd lived in Jack's shadow for so long . . . how could she be the destined one? She needed to know more, and the only one giving her any answers was her aunt. Maddie got up and walked into the kitchen.

Lisa stood when Maddie entered the room. "Are you all right?"

Maddie shrugged and sat at the table between Lisa and Erin. "I don't know," she sighed. "I'm not saying I believe any of this, but I want to know more."

Lisa and Erin exchanged a knowing glance. "That's fine," Lisa said. "What can we tell you?"

"Well," Maddie began, "Uncle Benny said that mixing the realms could cause an imbalance in the world."

Erin jumped in. "That's not right; wizards have traveled between the realms without causing any disturbances. Benny came to you all the time in the non-magical realm and nothing happened."

Lisa put her hand on top of Maddie's. "We believe that a magical rule will restore balance."

"And how is there no balance now?" Maddie inquired.

"Look at the non-magical realm," Erin explained. "All the non-magical technology that people have developed to become almost magical has destroyed that realm. The air and the water are polluted, the natural resources are being used up at an alarming rate, and no one in the non-magical realm can find a way to stop it."

"You think that a magical ruler can fix all that?" Maddie asked.

"Yes!" Lisa answered emphatically. "We can make magic available to that realm and do away with all the things that have ruined it."

"But non-magical people will be freaked out by the wizards," Maddie pointed out.

"At first," Erin reasoned. "But when we begin to better their lives and their living conditions, they will accept magic."

"Uncle Benny said that dreams and ideas will die if non-magical people were exposed to magic," Maddie said.

"You've been exposed to magic," Erin pointed out. "You've come up with a lot of ideas right here, and I don't think your dreams have died. Have they?"

Maddie shook her head. "You're asking me to accept a lot of things on your word. I need proof."

Lisa and Erin looked at each other again. "We can do that," Erin said.

"But it will be a long process," Lisa added.

"We can show you what a world run by magic would look like, but it will only be something of the imagination," Erin explained. "It won't be real; only something that *could* be. And it will take a very long time."

Maddie shrugged. "I have time and I have to know."

Lisa stood. "Very well, we will begin the journey then."

Jack

Jack spent most of the afternoon surfing through The Hawk's website. It showed videos of a man in his mid-twenties who appeared to be a fan of Goth wear. He had long, straight, jet-black hair, dark eyes accented with heavy eyeliner, and wore all black. There were several videos of his magic feats. One video showed The Hawk in a city park. He stopped a woman carrying a backpack and asked if he could hold it. Then, he asked the woman to concentrate on her greatest fear. The Hawk stared hard at her, waved his hand over the bag, and when he opened it, pulled out a large snake.

There were other videos that showed The Hawk levitating. One showed him hovering above a town pool, another over a bus, and one where he stepped out of a helicopter several hundred feet in the air and floated to the ground. Jack looked closely at these images, but he couldn't see where the cable was connected—though he knew there had to be one.

Some of the videos showed The Hawk swallowing various objects such as a pin and thread, and removing them from different parts of his body. The pin he pulled from his stomach and the thread from his eye. It was gross to watch, but Jack had seen enough "magic" over the last couple of months to know there was a trick behind all of it. Then, one video captured his attention.

The Hawk stood inside a store and approached the large storefront window. He put his hands against the glass, took several deep breaths, and then stepped through the glass and onto the sidewalk outside the store. Again, Jack knew there had to be a trick behind it, but he couldn't see where. He glanced out the window of the library and noticed that the sun was going down. He packed up his laptop, pulled the hood of his sweatshirt over his head, and headed home.

Once back in the house, Jack made himself another turkey sandwich and went to the basement, used a neighbor's unprotected WIFI connection he had previously stumbled upon, and continued to study the videos of The Hawk in action.

The advertisements were right: the tricks he saw were mind blowing, but nothing compared to the magic he and Maddie had performed. He'd have loved to see The Hawk make a giant bird explode, or project an image of himself to another place. That was *real* magic; no tricks behind those. Still, something about this magician kept Jack mesmerized.

At the end of one of the videos was an advertisement, stating that The Hawk would be performing at the Grand Avenue Theatre on July twenty-ninth. Jack looked at the calendar on the laptop. Today was the twenty-ninth. He checked the show times. There were two: eight p.m. and ten p.m. If he hurried, he could make it to the ten o'clock show.

The Grand Avenue Theatre was at the border of the county and the city line—a thirty-minute drive. But Jack didn't drive, so he did the only thing he could. He walked outside in the dark, closed his eyes, and when he opened them was a block from the theatre.

As Jack walked toward the theatre, he could see people standing in line for the show. Some of them were dressed in the same gothic garb he had seen The Hawk wear in his videos. There were several young women sharing videos of The Hawk on their smart phones and they giggled as they talked about how cute he was. A few street magicians were entertaining the crowd with tricks any kid could learn from a dollar store magic kit.

One of the magicians stopped Jack as he walked by. "Hey, kid!" he called. "Check this out."

This plea of "watch me" caught the attention a few people waiting in line. Jack watched as the man took out a wool ski cap and made an elaborate display of showing that it was empty. He then folded the hat, twirled it around in his hands, and produced a small bird from it. The watchers clapped, but Jack had seen what they missed. The bird was removed from an oversized jacket sleeve and quickly placed under the hat. Jack shrugged at the trick.

"What's the matter, kid?" the magician asked. "Do you think you can do better?"

Jack put out his hand. "Let me see the bird."

The magician handed over the bird, and Jack closed his eyes. He held the bird in both hands and began to squeeze his hands together—gently at first, and then tighter and tighter. Several of the onlookers started to squirm uncomfortably as Jack squeezed harder.

Finally, the magician couldn't take anymore. "Hey, kid!" he yelled. "You're killing the bird."

Jack opened his eyes and smiled at the magician. He made a motion as if he was throwing the bird at the magician, but when Jack opened his hands, the bird was gone. The small crowd clapped, and Jack started to walk away.

"How did you do that?" the magician begged.

Jack winked at him. "Magic," he said, and continued walking away.

In front of him, Jack saw a few teenagers selling tee shirts, and then, the person he was looking for. His father had taken him to several ballgames, and he'd been to the circus at this very arena a few times. So, he remembered there was always someone walking around, asking if anyone needed tickets. When a young man with a shaved head walked by and said, "Tickets," Jack knew he had found his man.

"Buying or selling?" Jack asked.

The man stooped, looked Jack over, and checked the surrounding area quickly. "How many?"

"Just one," Jack said. "The cheapest you got."

The man reached into a pocket inside his jacket and took out two tickets. "You sure you only need one?"

"Yeah, how much is it?"

"Sixty."

"For the worst seats you have?"

"You want it or not?"

Jack gave the man the money, who did a disappearing act of his own. He looked at the ticket and shook his head over having just spent sixty dollars on a thirty-dollar ticket. He'd have to be more careful with money; he was running out of it.

It took nearly half an hour of waiting in line, but Jack finally took his seat in the arena and, contrary to what he'd thought, the seat wasn't that bad. He was right at the center of the stage and about halfway to the top—not bad at all. Jack began to look around to see any props on the stage that would aid The Hawk's magic show, but he didn't see anything out of the ordinary. Pretty soon, the lights went down, loud music rocked the walls, and a heavy fog filled the stage. When it cleared, standing in the middle, dressed in black from head to toe, and sporting a long cape, was The Hawk. He started the magic act right away. The Hawk took off his cape, shook it hard, and several doves flew out of it and into the rafters.

Over the next ninety minutes, Jack watched carefully as The Hawk performed various tricks. He produced things he asked volunteers to think hard about from mid-air, he escaped from a straightjacket while upside down in a tank of water, and he made scribbles turn into the objects they represented. Very impressive. Jack tried to see where the trick was in every illusion, but even after studying magic for the last few months, he couldn't find a flaw in The Hawk's execution. The only thing he noticed was that before every trick, The Hawk waved his hand, which made Jack wonder if the magic The Hawk performed was more than just a trick.

For his last trick, The Hawk took a hard run from the very back of the stage, and just when it looked like he would run right into the audience, he pushed off the ground hard and took flight. The Hawk circled the arena and flew right over Jack. And even though he looked hard, Jack couldn't see any wires. The Hawk landed back on the stage to wild applause, and Jack was convinced: The Hawk was a wizard.

Maddie

Erin and Lisa led Maddie from the house and into the backyard. It seemed strange to Maddie that the yard reminded her of her own. She had no idea why she assumed the house of a wizard would have a yard that would be vastly different than those belonging to non-magical people, but she had, and the similarities surprised her. It had a well-kept lawn, a fence, and even a flower garden.

Lisa stood on one side of Maddie with Erin on the other. "Now," Lisa explained. "I'm going to cast a spell that will allow us to travel through the different realms of existence, but these realms are not reality; they are only what *can be* if ruled by magic. To us, the journey will be fast, but we will actually be gone for some time."

"So, everything I see won't be real?" Maddie asked.

"No," Erin answered. "It is only what can be, but it hasn't happened yet. Everything we see in these realms is a potential, and no one there will be able to see or hear you."

"That's right," Lisa went on. "We are only observers of a possibility. But we want you to see the truth of what a world ruled by magic would be like for everyone."

Maddie nodded. "I understand."

"Then we're ready?" Erin said.

Lisa lifted her hands and the wind began to blow around them. A small cyclone formed across the yard and moved towards them. The cyclone came closer and disturbed nothing; it simply encircled the three women, and they were lifted from the ground. It seemed like only a second later that they were being set down, and the cyclone vanished.

Maddie looked around. The surroundings were familiar, but the air seemed crisper than she was used to. The sun seemed to shine a little brighter, and things were more peaceful. She looked at the building across the street and realized that she was standing in front of her school. Several kids her age and younger were going into the school, but there were no buses or cars dropping them off. They seemed to be appearing out of nowhere.

Erin leaned toward Maddie. "I assume you recognize this place." Maddie nodded. "This is what the non-magical realm could be like under a magical rule," Erin said. "Have you noticed how clear the air is and how quiet and peaceful things are?"

Maddie nodded again.

"There will be no need for non-magical means of transportation," Lisa pointed out. "The pollution caused by those machines will cease, and nature will become the beautiful, pristine thing it was intended to be."

Maddie hardly heard a word Lisa said. She saw a girl her own age walking toward the school. The girl had long, straight, red hair and was very tall and thin. "Terry!" Maddie called, taking a step toward the girl.

Lisa stopped her. "Maddie, no one here can see you or hear you. This is only a world that could exist; it's not real."

Maddie hung her head and sighed as her friend went into the school. "I remember."

Lisa put an arm around Maddie. "I understand that you miss your friends," she said. "But you can make their lives better."

Maddie wanted to be sure she understood what she was seeing. "So the pollution is cleaned up by magical means . . . why doesn't that throw off the natural balance of things?"

"Do you really think that restoring the environment in the non-magical realm would upset the balance of the world?" Erin asked. "Doesn't it make more sense that doing away with pollution would restore the balance?"

Maddie didn't say anything. She *did* agree that it would be better if there was less pollution, and she agreed that preserving the environment was probably more in line with the true balance of the world, but that didn't mean she agreed with Tardon or his followers. How could she after they had kidnapped her parents? But Lisa had explained that that was the only way Tardon could make sure Maddie would return to the magical realm.

No, she thought. Even if Tardon only wanted to get her back to the magical realm, what about what he had done to the Gnomes? Tardon had destroyed their forest. But Lisa had said that the Gnomes brought the attack upon themselves. The Gnomes had kept certain animals out of the forest, away from their natural homes; the animals had only been trying to return to their rightful habitat. They were simply fighting to take back what they had been denied. It had nothing to do with Tardon. Was that right? Was everything Lisa said true? Maddie began to realize that it all came down to one thing: did she trust her Aunt Lisa?

Jack

Outside the theatre, Jack made his way to the stage door where all the hardcore fans were waiting for The Hawk. The crowd was made up of mostly high school girls and wannabe magicians who wanted a picture, an autograph, or, the Holy Grail: a chance to *touch* The Hawk. Jack definitely didn't fit in with this group, but he needed to talk to The Hawk, now that he was sure The Hawk was a wizard.

It had been a while since Jack had seen his family and he had no idea what had become of them after the battle with Tardon. He knew his mother was hurt, but Stanton had said she'd be fine, and Jack hoped that was true. But even if it was, wouldn't she, at least, have tried to make contact with him? Jack had thought that, by leaving the magical realm, he would have enticed his family to do the same. That hadn't happened, however. Even so, he had to leave.

He resented being thrown into a magical world and being forced to be something he knew nothing about. He wanted to choose his own future, but, according to what Tardon had told Jack, his future had already been decided. He and Maddie were *The Destined Ones*. They were destined to stop Tardon's attempt to take over all the realms of existence—something that would cause a great imbalance and the ultimate destruction of the world. According to Benny, that was. Jack didn't know if that was true; he'd only heard it from one source. Now, in The Hawk, Jack found a wizard who had obviously left the magical realm. Maybe The Hawk could give Jack some answers . . . answers he didn't get from Benny.

The back door opened, and two large men cleared the crowd of girls rushing forward to get a close up look at The Hawk. The men made a path from the door to a waiting limousine and, when The Hawk stepped outside, a couple of the girls actually screamed. The bodyguards held back the group as it moved forward and began shoving pictures, t-shirts, and magazines toward The Hawk for him to sign. He obliged as much of the crowd as he could in the few seconds it took him to walk to the car. One of the guards opened the car door, and The Hawk waved and thanked the crowd.

But just before he got in, Jack called out, "Hawk, I need to talk to you!"

The Hawk looked in Jack's direction. "Sorry, kid. I have to go."

Before The Hawk could get into the car, Jack closed his eyes and floated several feet into the air. The crowd gasped as Jack floated toward The Hawk and landed gently on the roof of the car. The Hawk looked at Jack, his eyes wide and his mouth open. The crowd broke into applause.

"I need to talk to you," Jack whispered. "I know where you're from and I know what you are."

The Hawk looked around and whispered to Jack through clenched teeth. "Take a bow."

Jack looked at the crowd and realized they were clapping for *him*. He waved and jumped off the car, landing very gently beside The Hawk. Immediately, one of the bodyguards moved toward Jack, but The Hawk held out his hand.

"Get in the car, kid," The Hawk said, and Jack got into the back of the limo. The Hawk got in after him and closed the door.

Jack had never been in a limo before and he was not impressed. It was big, and the seats were leather and very soft, but it smelled like an old ashtray and it needed a good scrubbing.

However, Jack wasn't here to enjoy the surroundings, and The Hawk reminded him of that as the limo pulled away from the theatre.

"Okay, kid," The Hawk said. "What are you up to?"

Jack shrugged. "I'm not up to anything. I just wanted to know why a wizard left the magical realm to be a famous magician here."

The Hawk laughed. "A wizard? Kid, there's no such thing as wizards."

"Right," Jack said. "And all those tricks you do that no other magician can do are just because you're such a great magician. And I just floated over your car a few minutes ago because I'm a great magician, too. I might be young, but I'm not stupid."

The Hawk looked out the window, took a deep breath, and turned back to Jack. "Okay, you got me. So, what do you want from me?"

"Exactly what I said before: I just want to know why you left the magical realm."

"I could ask you the same thing," The Hawk countered.

"Well, I'm not really from the magical realm," Jack explained. "I was raised here, so I just came home."

"You're a wizard. How can you not be from the magical realm?"

"I grew up here, like a normal kid. Me and my sister didn't know about the wizard thing until a few months ago."

The Hawk looked at Jack for a long time and seemed to working out a difficult math problem in his head. "You have a sister?"

Jack knew The Hawk was beginning to figure things out. "Yes," he said, and threw The Hawk a big clue. "I have a *twin* sister."

The Hawk leaned back and stared at Jack. "You're one of *The Destined Ones*."

Though he hated to hear the words, Jack nodded.

The Hawk's eyes went wide. "Now I get it. You came to find out why I'm here because you think I'm helping Tardon."

Jack shook his head. "Not exactly. I found you by accident, and when I figured out you were a wizard, I just wanted to talk to you. But . . . since you brought it up . . ."

"I'm not here to aid Tardon's cause," The Hawk insisted. "I'm actually here to get away from him. I never wanted to get involved in the conflict, and I told that to the Tars when they tried to recruit me, but they were having none of it. Because I didn't join them, they assumed I'd joined Stanton and they put an order out for my death. Stanton would have been fine with me staying neutral, but Tardon is forcing everyone to make a choice. His side or die. He won't let anyone be neutral."

"That's not true," Jack said. "There are neutral wizards."

"Not that I've heard of."

"My father's sister, Lisa—she's neutral."

"Are you talking about Lisa Baxter?" The Hawk asked. "You better start learning who's on your side and who's not. Lisa Baxter is definitely not neutral. Her husband was Tardon's number one, and since he died, she's stepped right into that role. Lisa Baxter is Tardon's top follower."

Maddie

Maddie looked at her school and thought about some of the lessons she had learned inside that building—things other than the usual reading, writing, and arithmetic. She'd been taught the importance of sharing, she'd studied the value of friendship, and she had been introduced to the mystery of trust. Trust was a subject first studied on the playground in kindergarten when the secret of who had cooties was whispered into the ear of a friend. If that person didn't tell the secret, then they were someone who could be trusted. But the trust issue confronting Maddie now held a great deal more of importance than which five-year-old boy had cooties. This trust issue could mean life or death.

Erin and Lisa stood on either side of Maddie again, which brought her out of her thoughts.

"We have more to see," Lisa said. And, once again, the silent cyclone engulfed them. In what seemed like seconds, they were lifted up and set down.

This time, they were in a large city. A city Maddie recognized. She'd been here before; her parents had taken her and Jack here at Christmas to see the big tree, and she'd been here to see a play on a school field trip, but something about it was different. It was much quieter than Maddie remembered and, when she looked around, she remembered that it was because in this version of the non-magical realm, there were no cars, buses, or trucks. The streets and the sidewalks were also much cleaner than she recalled, and she saw the reason why: on each corner were two people dressed in blue jumpsuits, holding brooms.

"You see," Erin pointed out. "The buses and taxis have been eliminated, so those in the transportation industry have been given jobs on the cleaning crews. They keep New York City spotless and are still able to provide for their families."

"So then magic doesn't provide everything people need?" Maddie asked.

Lisa took over the explanation. "The financial structures of the non-magical realm have remained in place. People still have to purchase goods and pay their bills. We are not looking to take over the world; we just want to make it a better place to live in."

Maddie looked around again. She remembered that the last time she had come to the city, she'd seen a few people begging for money and rooting around in garbage cans. She later found out that they were homeless people, and it was a big problem—not just in the cities, but everywhere. She'd felt sorry for these people. It bothered her that they had to sleep in the streets and eat what others had thrown away, but she didn't see any signs of the homeless now.

"I remember seeing homeless people when I was in the city before," Maddie said. "I don't see any now."

Erin smiled. "Without having to fund mass transportation, governments have been able to use their extra resources on social issues and have been providing education and health services to the homeless. They've also been able to provide people with affordable housing and jobs. Even the level of crime has been reduced."

Maddie scratched her head. "Crime has been eliminated through magic?"

"Oh, no. There is no magical way to change the nature of people, but governments have been able to use their extra resources to expand their security forces and prevent criminal activity."

It all sounded almost too good to be true. The air and the streets were clean, and people were being provided things they'd been previously denied. It seemed that Lisa was right; a magical rule was better for everyone, at least in this realm.

"So," Maddie said. "If the non-magical realm is such a great place, and everyone's needs are being met, doesn't that mean there's no reason for anyone to come up with new ideas?"

Lisa shook her head. "Not at all. Let's take, for example, what you call *technology*. Your cell phones, computers, and such. Magic has no need to get involved in any of that. We have no need for those inventions, but non-magical people do, and they will continue to come up with ways to improve on those devices."

"What about dreams?"

"What about them?" Erin asked. "We've shown you that under a magical rule, the non-magical world would be a better place to live in—a better place to dream about the future, a better place for children to have fantasies, to play unbounded. Dreams will flourish, and non-magical people will dream like never before because their dreams can come true."

"People will always dream," Lisa added. "Children will dream of faraway places and fantastic adventures, young lovers will dream of marriage and future families, and parents will dream of the wonderful things their children can become."

"So, the dream world won't die—like Uncle Benny said it would?"

Lisa put an arm around Maddie. "Of course not. All that will happen is that people's dreams will have a greater chance of coming true."

Maddie smiled. This version of the non-magical realm certainly seemed to be a much better place than the one she left. She definitely liked what she'd seen, but why did they need her? Why was she the one to lead the magical realm to the forefront?

"Okay," she said. "I can see that the world will be a better place with magic, but why can't you do all of this without me?"

Lisa smiled. "Because of your strength. It is destined that all of this be built on a rock. You are the rock; you have the strength needed to accomplish all of this."

Maddie bit her bottom lip and shook her head. "I don't understand."

"Maddie," Lisa continued. "In order to unite the realms under magic, it is necessary for one with great power and influence to rule. Tardon has spread the word, but he cannot unite everyone; even he realizes this. You've come from the non-magical realm, and you have influence with very powerful wizards who have chosen the wrong side. Only you can show everyone the way. All this good can only be accomplished through *you*. It is destined."

Maddie wasn't sure she fully understood, but everything she had seen looked very good. She wanted people to live healthy, happy lives. She wanted to ensure the future for all. Maddie took a deep breath and let it out slowly. She decided that she would trust her Aunt Lisa and step up to take the place she was destined for.

Jack

The limo pulled into the back of a large hotel and right up to a door marked "Employee Entrance." Another crowd was waiting, though not as large as the one outside the theatre. Jack wondered how it was that The Hawk was so popular, yet he had never heard of him. Then again, Jack had been preoccupied recently and never really had an interest in magic until it was forced on him.

The Hawk leaned toward Jack. "When the door opens, don't stop. Just follow my man right into the hotel, to the service elevator, and up to the room. We'll talk there."

Jack nodded, and when the car door opened, he stepped out first with The Hawk right behind him. Several people yelled, trying to get The Hawk's attention and, normally, he would have waved and sign some autographs, but not tonight. The Hawk simply put his head down and followed his bodyguard and Jack into the hotel.

They walked down a gray concrete hallway and passed doors marked "Men's Locker Room," "Women's Locker Room," and "Laundry Room," to an open elevator. They all stepped inside and, when the doors closed, went all the way to the top floor: the penthouse suite.

The Hawk's guard opened the door to the suite, looked around inside, and then waved in The Hawk and Jack.

The Hawk slapped the guard on his shoulder. "Thanks, Marcus," he said. "That's all for tonight."

Marcus nodded, looked hard at Jack as if giving him a warning, and then left.

Jack had been on family vacations before, and he knew what

a hotel room was supposed to look like, but this was no economy lodge just outside Disney World with a dripping faucet and an air conditioner that worked when it felt like it. No, this was a *luxury* hotel room.

The entry door opened to a large living room, where a black leather couch sat along one wall and a large, flat screen T.V. hung on the opposite wall. A small bar took up a corner of the room, and sliding glass doors opened to a balcony. The Hawk walked behind the bar while Jack stood at the door, gaping at the room.

"You want something, kid?" The Hawk asked, bringing Jack out of his state of awe.

"Do you have a Coke?"

"Sure." The Hawk took out two sodas from a small refrigerator. He handed one to Jack as he walked past him, sat on the couch, and invited Jack to sit.

Jack moved to one of the chairs next to the couch. He opened the soda, took a long sip, and let out a small burp.

The Hawk opened his own soda and leaned back on the couch. "So, you're one of *The Destined Ones*."

Jack decided that he'd be the one to ask the questions. "What else do you know about Lisa?"

The Hawk swallowed another sip of soda. "Look, kid, that's one lady you don't need to know about."

"First," Jack said. "My name's Jack, not *kid*. And second, I need to know as much about her as possible—believe me."

The Hawk put his soda can on the coffee table. "I only know what I've heard."

Jack inched forward in his seat. "So, tell me what you've heard."

"Well," The Hawk said. "She's not a very nice lady."

Jack rolled his eyes. "I know that much. I want to know about her relationship with Tardon."

The Hawk leaned back. "She's been very active in recruiting for Tardon. She has this power to communicate with animals and she uses it to bring some of the fiercest beasts in the magical realm under Tardon's influence."

"So it was Tardon who attacked the Gnomes," Jack said, almost to himself.

"What's that?"

"The Forest Gnomes were recently attacked by dragons and giant bears," Jack informed him.

"The Gici Awas."

"The Gici what?" Jack asked.

"The Gici Awas are fierce, giant bears, and if they are under Tardon's control, it won't be good for anyone," The Hawk answered. "The Forest Gnomes have tried for centuries to control them because of their destructive nature, but if Tardon has set them loose, they could wipe out the Gnomes."

"Why would Tardon want to destroy the Gnomes?"

"Because the Gnomes have not joined his side," The Hawk explained. "That's not something Tardon takes lightly. Anyone who hasn't taken his side he considers an enemy, and Tardon will do all he can to destroy his enemies."

Jack took another sip of soda. "I don't get it. Why would someone want to rule so much that he'd kill people to do it?"

The Hawk smiled. "That's good, Jack. The fact that you don't understand means you're not like them, which is exactly how you need to be to stop them."

"Why hasn't anyone stopped him yet?"

"Many have tried—Stanton harder than anyone else. But

Tardon is a very powerful wizard and he surrounds himself with other powerful wizards."

Jack leaned back in his seat. "Then how are me and my sister supposed to beat him if no one else can?"

"Because it's destined," The Hawk replied.

Jack shook his head. "You're not funny."

The Hawk sighed. "I'm sorry. I'm not trying to be funny. It's just that the story says only one with the power of two can defeat Tardon, and . . ."

"That means twins," Jack finished. "I know that much, but why?"

"No one's told you?"

"No one tells me anything," Jack said. "That's why I left."

"You have to go back," The Hawk said.

Jack raised his voice. "Why?"

"Because it's destined."

Jack leapt to his feet. "Stop saying that!"

"But that's the reason!" The Hawk yelled back.

"Tell me why!"

The Hawk let out a long breath. "Okay. Have a seat, calm yourself, and I'll tell you what I've heard."

Jack looked at him, searching his eyes for any sign of deceit. "Really?" The Hawk nodded, and Jack returned to his seat.

The Hawk took another drink from his can of soda. "I have no idea why no one's told you this. It seems that the ones destined to defeat Tardon should have as much information as possible, but what do I know?"

"Can you get on with it?" Jack urged.

"Okay. This is only a story, and no one knows if it's true or not, but here it is. It's said that only one with the power of two can defeat Tardon . . ."

"Twins," Jack interrupted. "But why?"

"Because Tardon himself is a twin."

Jack jumped to his feet again. "There's another one like him?!"

The Hawk shook his head. "No, and please sit down."

Jack took a deep breath and sat.

"The story is," The Hawk continued, "that Tardon was born a twin, but his twin died while still in the womb. The great power Tardon has comes from his twin."

Jack scratched his head. "I'm not sure I get it."

"Whatever magical power Tardon's twin would have possessed was transferred to Tardon before the twin died. So . . ."

"Tardon has the power of two," Jack said.

"Yes," The Hawk said. "But since there are no wizard twins, not many people believed the story until . . ."

"Me and Maddie."

"That's why people began to believe you and your sister were *The Destined Ones,* and that's why Tardon went searching for you."

"That's why we were brought to the non-magical realm," Jack said. "Mom and Dad were protecting us."

"It's also why you have to go back. If Stanton's right, and Tardon takes over all the realms of existence, the world will be destroyed."

"Do you think Stanton's right?" Jack asked.

"I'm not sure he's ever been wrong. And, according to him, only you and your sister can stop Tardon."

"Well, then, we have a problem," Jack said.

"What's that?"

Jack sighed. "I have no idea where my sister is."

Maddie

Maddie, Lisa, and Erin were once again lifted up inside the small cyclone, and when they were set down, Maddie saw that they were inside what looked like a large cave. The rock walls, gravel floor, cool damp air, and musty old basement smell reminded her of the cave of the Forest Gnomes. She looked around, expecting to be greeted by Togo and his mother, Fala, but instead, two red-hooded figures emerged from a dark side of the cave.

Lisa and Erin immediately greeted the two figures and, after a few seconds, Lisa waved Maddie over. The two hooded figures turned, and Maddie, Lisa, and Erin followed them into the darkness from where they came. They walked down a long, rock-lined corridor and, a few times, Maddie stumbled on the pebbles that made up the path. After several minutes of walking, they emerged into a room that she thought looked like a large living room. A fireplace was on the wall across from the entrance, and a large fire raged within. On either side of the fireplace were large chairs, each with a small table beside it. Across from the chairs, its back facing the entrance where Maddie stood, was a leather couch, and between the couch and chairs was a large circular table that completed the sitting area.

Scattered around the room were small tables and chairs where several red-cloaked people sat, engaged in conversation. As Maddie looked around, the two hooded figures that had led them to the room lowered their hoods. Both were young men in their twenties. One of them addressed Lisa.

"Please, make yourselves comfortable," he said. "We will bring you some refreshments."

"Thank you," Lisa said, and the two men disappeared into the darkness on one side of the cave.

Lisa led the way to an open table just to the left of the fireplace. She, Erin, and Maddie sat down, and Maddie was still looking around the room.

"What is this place?" Maddie asked.

"It's a meeting place for our cause," Lisa replied.

Maddie continued her questioning. "And where are we?"

"Inside one of the mountains," Lisa answered. "With so many still misunderstanding our true intentions, it's best that we stay hidden until we can properly spread our message."

One of the young men returned, carrying a tray with a plate of bread and cheese, a pitcher of water, and three glasses. He set down the refreshments, bowed, and left.

Lisa filled the three glasses, cut a piece of bread for herself, and addressed Maddie. "What do you think of what we can do for the world?"

Maddie swallowed a small sip of water. "I think it can be a good thing for everyone. If that's what can really happen."

Erin took a bite of cheese and washed it down with a gulp of water. "Of course it's really what can happen—but only if we can overcome the obstacles."

Maddie looked down for a moment. Then she glanced at Erin. "You mean Stanton."

"Oh, no," Lisa said. "I don't think Stanton could ever be convinced; his hatred of Tardon is too great, and he'd never admit that he was wrong. It's the other wizards—the ones that haven't made up their minds that need convincing—and that's where you'll be able to show your leadership abilities."

Maddie's eyes narrowed a bit. "How am I going to do that?"

"By getting out and talking to them," Erin said.

"You want me to go out and make speeches?" Maddie blinked.

Lisa smiled. "No. Not right away. We'll start by visiting the homes of some of the undecided and see how well you do."

Maddie studied Erin and Lisa's expressions. "You're not kidding, are you?"

"Of course not," Erin said. "If you're going to lead a movement this important, you'd better be able to talk to people about it."

Lisa moved her chair closer to Maddie and took her hand. "I know it's a lot to take in, but I see the strength in you, and I know that what has been said about you is true. You're all we've hoped for: a bridge between the magic and non-magic realms, the solid foundation we need to lead us. Tardon has laid the groundwork, but it is *you* who will make sure that all we've hoped for comes to be." Lisa looked at Maddie for a few seconds. "I know you have doubts," she continued, "but I will be here for you, for whatever you need."

Maddie looked down and noticed her shaking hands. "You're sure it has to be me?"

"Your place has been destined"

"I hope you're right."

Lisa smiled. "Good. Now I have to see someone. Are you all right?"

Maddie nodded.

"Okay then, you stay with Erin, and I'll be right back."

Lisa walked to the dark area of the room where the two greeters were still standing. She stopped in front of them and asked, "Is he waiting?"

"Yes," the shorter of the two answered.

She then walked down a long corridor that was lit by torches hanging on the walls. She stopped in front of a large wooden door, took a deep breath, and knocked.

A familiar voice called from the other side of the door. "Enter!"

Lisa pushed open the heavy door and walked into a small room. A fire pit in the center of the room was lit, and the dancing flames cast a dim, shadowy light that made it difficult to see the figure in red standing across the room.

"Come in, Lisa," the hooded person said.

She pushed the door closed behind her and walked across the room. "She's ready."

The figure lowered his hood, and long, white hair fell around his face. His cold, gray eyes bore into Lisa's, and she resisted the temptation to look away.

"Very good," Tardon said. "And what about her brother?"

"We've kept Maddie away for some time, and she's had no contact with him," Lisa answered. "As far as we know, he's left the magical realm."

"Good. It is important that we keep them apart until Stanton's guard is destroyed. After that, not even *The Destined Ones* will be able to stop us."

"Shall we proceed with the initiation?"

"Yes," he said. "We must make her feel that she is part of the family." Tardon walked close to Lisa and put a hand on her shoulder. "You've done very well. Now, keep the girl close to you; she must trust you completely."

"I believe she does."

Tardon smiled. "Good, very good."

Jack

The Hawk stared at Jack for a long time. A couple of times, he started to say something, but the words wouldn't come, so he just shook his head.

"I know what you're thinking," Jack said.

The Hawk shook his head again. "You might think so, but I doubt you do."

Jack looked at The Hawk. "You're wondering how I could lose track of my sister, especially since we're twins. And you're thinking: *what am I doing here when I have so much to do?*" He paused and looked into The Hawk's eyes. "Am I right?"

The Hawk returned Jack's gaze. "Yes and no. I am definitely wondering how you lost track of your sister. I mean, you two are *The Destined Ones*; you have to stay together."

"We didn't know we were *The Destined Ones*. No one ever told us, and I don't think Maddie even knows about this 'destiny' thing."

The Hawk hung his head. "How is that possible?"

Jack stood up and walked to the sliding glass doors that led to the balcony. He looked at the lights of the city and the moon shining in the sky. "It's a long story."

The Hawk got up and stood beside him. "I have time, kid. Maybe you should tell it to me."

Jack nodded as he continued to stare at the night sky. "I guess I should." He returned to his seat. The Hawk followed and sat back on the couch.

Jack looked at the floor while he recounted for The Hawk how Tardon had kidnapped his parents and how Benny had brought him and Maddie to the magical realm. He conveyed the journey to find his parents and the battle with the Tars. Jack explained that no one had ever once mentioned anything about him and Maddie being *The Destined Ones*. It was only after he and Maddie were separated that Jack had learned of his destiny—and from a very unlikely source.

"Wait a minute," The Hawk said. "It was Tardon who told you about your destiny? Your family never mentioned it to you?"

Jack continued to look at the floor. "They never said a word; that's part of the reason I left." He looked at The Hawk. "After my mother was hurt, and Lisa disappeared with Maddie, I didn't want anything to do with any of them, or the magical realm but . . ." Jack stopped and ran his hands through his hair. "I guess I have to go back."

The Hawk nodded. "Yeah, you do, but not alone."

Jack's eyes opened wide as he spoke. "You really want to do that?! You don't even know me. Why would you do that?"

"And they say I'm full of myself," The Hawk muttered. "What makes you think I'm doing it for you? The magical realm is my home, and if I can help save it, I will."

Jack scratched his head. "I don't get it—you left the magical realm."

"Yeah, I did. I left to save my own life; I was afraid and I'm not proud of it. You made me see that this thing is bigger than just one person."

Jack smiled. Even though he knew The Hawk would be in danger, he was glad that he wouldn't be alone. "I really should stop at home first."

"I have some preparations of my own to make." The Hawk got up and shook his long hair. "I'm a big star, you know. I can't just disappear."

Jack got to his feet as well. "Okay, you do what you have to do, and I'll take care of my stuff and—"

"I'll meet you at your place in the morning," The Hawk finished.

Jack looked at The Hawk, a little confused. "How will you know where to find me? You don't know where I live."

The Hawk smiled. "I think I'll be able to find you.

"Okay, if you can find me, then find me at eight in the morning."

Jack walked out on the balcony and looked over the lit city skyline. The Hawk followed. "I don't want you to feel like you have to go back, I mean . . ." While Jack's words trailed, he looked down for a second, thinking of what to say next. "I don't want anything to happen to you because of me."

"Kid," The Hawk started to say, but caught himself. "Sorry, I mean, *Jack*. I told you I'm not going back for you; I'm going back to try to save my home, and the world. It's the right thing to do."

"Even though Tardon wants you dead?"

The Hawk put a hand on Jack's shoulder. "Yes, even though Tardon wants me dead. But I'll be okay; I'll be with one of *The Destined Ones*."

Jack smiled. "That's true."

"Hey, Jack." The Hawk's face tensed. "I'm going to say this because you have to know that I'll never lie to you and I'll always tell it like it is."

Jack wasn't sure where this was going, but he felt slightly uncomfortable as The Hawk continued.

49

"You know it's not just me who Tardon wants dead."

"I know," Jack said. "Believe me, I know."

"Okay then. I'll see you in the morning."

"Bright and early," Jack reminded him. Then he closed his eyes and disappeared.

Jack

It was still dark when Jack appeared in his backyard, but he knew it was close to sunrise because the birds had already begun to chirp. He walked cautiously across the yard to his unlocked basement window and slipped inside. In a box beside the mattress in his sleeping corner, he had tucked away a few objects he'd made for self-defense. He knew that magic would be a fine defense, but if he could avoid using it, why give himself away as a wizard.

Inside the box was a set of homemade nunchucks—two thick sticks, about six inches long, with an eight-inch piece of rope tied between them. Not that Jack knew how to properly use them, but swinging them at someone would at least look intimidating and hurt a lot if he actually managed to hit someone. There was also a small plastic case that looked like a wallet. Inside were a dozen Chinese stars, which were basically large metal coins with very sharp points. When thrown at someone, these could cause a great deal of damage. Jack had practiced with these . . . *a lot*. He threw them from different distances at various targets he'd set up around the basement, and had become pretty good.

The sticks and the stars went right into his backpack. The box also contained a large metal pipe and a rope with a large knot on the end that he'd wrapped heavily in duct tape; these would have to stay, as they were too large for the backpack. Jack knew that where he was going he could openly use magic for self-defense, but it wouldn't hurt to have a few surprises.

Next, he grabbed a few books that would not be making it back to the library. A book of spells that Jack would have to verify for its usefulness, a book on famous wizards throughout history that only contained the names of characters from fairy tales (but he enjoyed reading it), and a history of magic through the years that might be useful if the information was authentic.

After packing, Jack walked around the house. He went into the living room where he'd spent uncountable hours playing games and watching movies with his family, who were now scattered who knew where. He paused in the kitchen, where endless numbers of meals were shared with his parents and Maddie. In his parents' bedroom, he smelled the faint remains of his mother's perfume and smiled. He went into his own bedroom and saw the stack of video games that hadn't been touched in some time, but those days were past him now.

Jack then made his way to his sister's room. He'd never really spent much time in there, but the light purple paint and the bubble-gum-colored blanket on the bed were pure Maddie. The books stacked neatly on the desk and the pens in their holder, standing watch like guards on night duty, reflected Maddie's studious nature. On the corner of the desk, Jack saw something he had never known Maddie had: a picture of the two of them. It had been taken at the beach, and the smiles on their faces said it had been a good day.

He picked up the picture and sat on the edge of Maddie's bed. He stared into it and felt water begin to build in his eyes. "Maddie," he begged. "Where are you?" He lay back on the bed and the tears began to flow freely.

A loud crash forced Jack's eyes open, and he sat up quickly. There was something—or someone—moving around the house. His first thought was that the investigators were back to gather evidence on the family's disappearance. Or, maybe, it was just someone from the water company finally showing up to turn off the water because no one had paid that bill in forever. Still, it could have been someone just breaking in to an abandoned house, hoping to find something of value.

Whatever it was, Jack didn't want to be seen. He got up and stood behind the bedroom door, listening—a skill that was now highly developed, thanks to many long nights lying in the basement and waiting for sleep to come. He could tell the difference between a footstep and a branch brushing along the side of the house. So, when he heard the shuffling, he knew, without a doubt, someone was in the house.

Jack peeked into the hallway, but there was no one there. Then he heard the shuffle of a footstep on the floor below and ducked back behind the door.

Okay, he thought. *There is someone here, but how do I deal with this intruder?* He could have simply hid and waited for the person to leave, which would have worked if it had been someone from the water company. But, what if it was an investigator poking around the house? They'd go into every room and look under every bed, and Jack would surely be discovered.

The shuffling footstep sounded again, and the noise was moving toward the stairs. Jack took a deep breath. He decided the best thing to do would be a blast of magic and a dash out the door before the trespasser knew what hit him. Jack heard the unmistakable sound of a creaking step. The stranger was coming his way, and he was ready.

Maddie's bedroom was the first room at the top of the stairs, so Jack listened closely to the footsteps as they moved toward him. He counted each footstep, knowing there were twelve steps to the top landing. His mouth went dry as the sounds got closer to the twelfth. When Jack counted twelve, the footsteps stopped. He burst from Maddie's room with his hands extended in front of him.

The force Jack sent out caught the intruder just as he reached the top of the stairs. He screamed Jack's name while he flew down the flight of stairs, his long black hair being tossed about. Jack heard his name and knew he'd made a mistake. The black-clad figure hit the bottom of the stairs with a sickening thud.

Jack ran down the stairs and knelt beside the fallen figure. "Hawk. Are you okay?"

The Hawk propped himself up against the wall and took in several deep breaths. "What'd you do that for?"

"I'm sorry. I thought someone broke in."

The Hawk struggled to his feet and Jack grabbed his arm to help. When he finally stood, The Hawk was still a bit wobbly, so he sat on the stairs. "Wow, kid, you really pack some power."

Jack heard The Hawk call him "kid," and wanted to stop him from saying it again, but this wasn't the time. Instead, he just said again, "I'm sorry."

"Don't be," The Hawk said while he got up and tried to shake off his minor injuries. "You're really strong—I'm glad I'm on your side."

Jack watched The Hawk swaying while trying to keep his feet beneath him. He looked pale, and Jack thought the poor guy might get sick at any moment.

"You sure you're okay?" Jack asked.

The Hawk nodded, but Jack wasn't buying it. "Why don't you sit back down?"

The Hawk didn't argue and sat down.

"I'll be right back," Jack said, leaving The Hawk alone.

He went downstairs to the basement and grabbed his backpack and a bottle of water from the cooler. He looked around the basement, sighed, and headed back upstairs.

As he walked from the basement to the stairs where The Hawk was sitting, Jack took another peek into each room as he passed. He looked at the kitchen again, saw the pictures hanging in the hallway, and kept walking to avoid the memories. He looked into the living room, the scene of his last happy moment in the house, the burn marks on the walls reminding him that it was also the scene of the most terrifying moment. Then he headed towards The Hawk.

The Hawk was on his feet when Jack returned. He looked steady and his normal coloring had come back. Jack took another glance at the living room.

"You okay, kid?" The Hawk asked.

Jack nodded. "Yeah, are you?"

"I'm fine," he replied as Jack handed him the water bottle. He drank half of the bottle in one gulp.

"You're sure you want to come with me?" Jack asked.

"I'm sure. It's time for me to do the right thing."

"Won't your fans miss you?"

The Hawk smiled. "I took care of that. It seems there's a family emergency that needs tending to, and The Hawk would appreciate privacy while he deals with a very difficult situation. At least, that's what the press release will say."

"Then I guess we're ready."

"Any particular place you want us to go?" The Hawk asked.

"I'll lead the way," Jack said. "I have a friend who will help us."

The Hawk held onto Jack's arm, Jack closed his eyes, and they vanished.

Maddie

Maddie and Erin hadn't said a word to each other since Lisa had left them. Why that was, Maddie didn't know, and it surprised her somewhat. They were close enough in age; Erin was maybe a couple of years older, so they should at least have been able to carry on a conversation—or so Maddie had thought. They didn't have to be best friends, but they could talk. Yet, for some reason, they didn't. Maddie had simply sat there, contemplating what she had seen. The world, unpolluted, uncongested—a peaceful, beautiful place. What Erin was thinking was anyone's guess.

Maddie caught Erin staring at her several times, and Maddie took her turn staring back. She thought Erin was very pretty. Her eyes were a greenish brown, her hair blonde and long. It fell naturally around her face like a frame around a beautiful painting. But something wasn't right. What was going on behind those pretty eyes? What was it that Erin was thinking about when she looked at Maddie? Did she see a potential friend, or did she see a threat? Was she jealous of the position Lisa said Maddie was to take? The position Lisa said Maddie was destined to. Could that be the reason for Erin's silence? And, was Maddie really the one destined to lead the magical realm to a place of prominence in the world?

Maddie took a deep breath and decided to ask Erin the questions that were dancing in her head. But, that would have to wait, because Lisa stepped out of the dark corner of the cave and into the large room where she'd left the two girls. She walked over to the table.

"Ladies," she said. "Let's get out of here and get ourselves cleaned up and rested."

Erin got to her feet quickly, as if she welcomed the occasion to be free of Maddie's company.

Maddie also stood. "And where are we going?"

"My house. Is that all right?"

Maddie looked at Erin who appeared to shake her head slightly.

"Why wouldn't it be?" Maddie asked.

"Okay, then," Lisa said. "Let's get going." She led the way back down the rock-lined corridor to the mouth of the cave where they'd first appeared. Lisa put out both hands, and Erin and Maddie each took one. Lisa closed her eyes, and they were gone.

They reappeared in Lisa's front yard, and Maddie looked around, her mouth opened wide. By the full moon, she could see that the grass was nearly knee-high, and the flowers were brown and losing their petals.

Lisa looked at Maddie. "Is there something wrong?"

"What happened to the yard? It was so nice."

Lisa and Erin exchanged smiles. "I should take care of that," Lisa said, and she waved her hand and the grass became neat and trimmed. The flowers perked up and were vibrant with color once more. "That's better." Lisa then opened the front door and led the way inside.

Erin sat down on the couch, and Maddie took a seat in a chair across from her while Lisa went into the kitchen.

"How did the yard get so overgrown so quickly?" Maddie said, almost to herself.

"We were gone for a while," Erin told her.

"It didn't feel like it," Maddie replied.

Lisa returned to the living room, carrying a plate of small sandwiches. She put the plate on the coffee table, along with some napkins. Before sitting on the couch beside Erin, she grabbed a sandwich.

"Actually," Lisa began to explain, "we were gone for more than several weeks. The spell I cast before we left made time pass quickly for us, or the trip would have been far too exhausting."

Maddie leaned back and sighed. "This magic thing is so confusing."

Lisa and Erin laughed.

"Don't worry, honey," Lisa said. "You'll get used to it."

Out of nowhere, thoughts of her family rushed into Maddie's head. "My parents, Jack . . . I need to see them."

"We'll have to make arrangements for that," Lisa said calmly as she stood. "But we'll do that in the morning. Right now, I think we could all do with some rest."

Maddie didn't argue; she was suddenly exhausted and some rest sounded good. She followed Lisa down the hall to a small bedroom. A bed leaned against the wall across from the door, and a small window was at the head of the bed. Lisa gave Maddie a quick hug and closed the door as she left the room.

Maddie went over to the window and looked outside. The full moon lit the yard like a spotlight. "I miss you, Mom and Dad," she whispered, and quickly added, "I miss you too, Jack." She turned away from the window, but quickly turned back. Something had caught her eye: a small figure—one that was somewhat familiar.

Maddie scanned the yard several times, paying close attention to the bushes lining the back of the yard, but saw nothing. She shrugged, turned from the window, and walked to the bed. She rubbed her eyes. It had been a long day, and fatigue was getting to her. Maddie kicked off her shoes, and lay back on the bed with her eyes closed.

From the bushes a figure emerged and stared at the window where Maddie had been seconds ago. Togo bowed his head and sighed.

"I fear you are making a grave mistake, Miss Maddie," he said.

Jack

Jack felt the soft, moist ground under his feet, and the strong smell of pine and cedar told him that he'd hit his mark. He opened his eyes and looked up at the tall trees. Some still showed signs of the recent attack, but the small leaves on the ends of the branches told him they were healing.

The Hawk had let go of Jack's arm and was looking around. "I thought we were going to see a friend of yours," he said. "What are we doing in the woods?"

Jack smiled and walked over to a large rock between two pine trees. "We *are* here to see a friend." He put his hand on the rock, not knowing if he'd be able to get it to open. He leaned close to the rock and whispered, "I need to see Chief Togo."

But nothing happened, and after several tries, Jack took his hand off the rock and turned to The Hawk. "I guess we'll just have to wait." He sat on the ground with his back against the large rock.

The Hawk sat next to him. "If you tell me what you're trying to do, maybe I can help. I have a little more experience at this wizard thing than you."

"Do you know how to get in touch with the Forest Gnomes?" Jack asked.

The Hawk moved back slightly "The Forest Gnomes," he said. "Those are the friends you wanted to see? You know, kid, they're not really friendly to wizards." He looked around the forest. "In fact, they don't really like us being in the forest at all. They think it belongs to them and that we don't know how to treat it with the proper respect."

"*Most* of you don't know how to treat the forest with respect," a small voice interrupted from beside the large rock.

Jack jumped to his feet and almost ran to the small female gnome standing in front of them. She was wearing a brown hiking outfit and had her hair tied back in a tight braid that stuck out from under a white kerchief she wore on her head. Jack stopped just before hugging her and reached out his hand instead.

"Fala!" he said. "It's great to see you." Jack wasn't just saying so; he really *was* glad to see Fala. He had no particular love for the magical realm, or anyone in it, but the Gnomes had gone out of their way to help him, risking their lives in the process. And he would never forget that. Fala and her son, Togo, had earned a special place in Jack's heart. He could never pay them back for all they'd done. But he could, and would, show them the utmost respect.

Fala took Jack's hand, and Jack, having seen a man greet a woman in this manner in a movie once, kissed her hand.

Fala smiled. "It's very nice to see you again, young one, especially considering what I've heard."

Jack took a step back. "And what have you heard?"

Fala bowed her head. "Forgive me," she said. "But it has been said that you left the magical realm, you turned your back on your family, and on your destiny, and . . ." She bowed again. "I find these words difficult to say, but it's being said that you have turned your back on all of us."

Jack had never thought about what he'd done as turning his back on anyone, but, having heard it, he guessed it was true. The realization of it hit him hard, and as his legs went weak, he stumbled back, bounced into a tree, and sat.

Fala and The Hawk moved quickly to his side. "Kid," The Hawk said. "Are you okay?"

Jack nodded, but didn't say anything. The words "turned your back on your family" kept repeating themselves over and over in his head. Then, the lesson that Connie had tried to teach him found room to manifest itself. *Control your emotions.* In anger, Jack had left the magical realm; he had turned his back on his family, his destiny, and everyone. He took a few deep breaths.

"I'm sorry," he said, looking into Fala's eyes. How could he explain to her why he'd done what he had? How could he explain it to any of the Gnomes after they had risked so much? He looked up at the remains of the burnt trees. They'd nearly given their home to help him, and he had just left them. But he was back now; maybe the *how* and *why* wouldn't matter.

"I guess it's true," Jack finally said. "I left the magical realm and my family." He paused and swallowed hard. "And, I left all of you. I'm sorry for that, but I'm back now, and I'm going to do the right thing."

Fala smiled. "I'm glad to hear that."

Jack saw Fala glance at The Hawk. "I'm sorry," he said. "Fala, this is . . ."

"Allan," The Hawk said, and he shook Fala's hand.

Jack looked at The Hawk. "*Allan?*"

"Yes, Allan," The Hawk replied. "What—did you think my parents named me *Hawk?*"

Jack lowered his head.

"You did!" The Hawk laughed. "You actually thought 'The Hawk' was my name!"

Jack looked up. "Shut up! You think my name is *kid.*"

The Hawk stopped laughing. "I'm sorry; if you want me to stop calling you that, I will."

Jack shook his head. "It's okay; don't worry about it."

Fala cleared her throat. "Well, Allan, it's very nice to meet you. Now, let's go inside."

The Hawk helped Jack to his feet, and Fala tapped the large rock. It split to reveal a large passageway. Fala entered, and Jack and The Hawk followed.

The damp, musty smell of the passageway made Jack feel oddly comfortable, and when Fala led them to the small cave Jack had stayed in previously, he actually felt at home.

"I will bring you something to eat," Fala said, and she left Jack and The Hawk.

Jack took off his backpack and sat on one of the rocks surrounding a small fire pit in the center of the room. Even in the summer, the cave was cool, but the fire kept it tolerable.

The Hawk sat beside Jack and asked, "What is this place?"

Jack smiled. "This is the home of the Forest Gnomes."

"And why are we here?"

"I can't just show up at Benny's," Jack explained. "I didn't leave there on the best of terms. The Gnomes helped me before, and I was hoping they would help me again."

"Do you want them to help you get in touch with your family?" The Hawk asked.

He looked into the fire. He really wanted help finding Maddie, but hearing The Hawk mention his family made Jack think that he should reach out to them. The last time he had seen his mother, she was badly injured, and the way he had spoken to his father was something Jack needed to apologize for. But Benny was a different matter. Jack had been harsh with him; of that there was no doubt. But Benny had withheld so much information from Jack that Jack didn't think he could trust Benny. In this case, Jack felt he was the one who deserved the apology. Even so, The Hawk was right: Jack needed to get in touch with his family.

Before Jack could answer The Hawk, Fala returned, carrying a large basket. She set it down beside the fire, spread out a blanket, and took out several different kinds of fruits, berries, and bread. She also took out a large jug and two wooden cups. Then she opened the jug and filled the cups with juice. Jack and The Hawk looked at each other for a second before they began to eat vigorously. Fala sat on a nearby rock and watched as they ate their fill.

Finally, Jack and The Hawk looked up from their feast, and each of them took a deep breath and a long drink from their cups.

The Hawk looked at Fala. "That was very good," he said. "Thank you."

Fala smiled and nodded.

"Yes," Jack chimed in. "Thank you very much, Fala."

"You're quite welcome, young sir," she said.

Jack took another gulp of juice. "Would it be possible to speak to Chief Togo?"

Fala sighed. "If he were here, I'm sure he'd like very much to speak to you, but as it is, he has been away."

"I guess he's pretty busy, now that he's Chief."

"I'm not sure," Fala said. "He told me he had a mission to fulfill, and I have been carrying out his duties as Chief."

Jack scratched his head. "He can do that? Just leave you in charge like that?"

"Well," Fala said, "one of his duties as Chief is to be a role model. By carrying out this mission, Togo is showing the importance of keeping one's word. He is leading by example." She stood up. "If you must speak to him, I will try to get a message to him. In the meantime, you and your friend are welcome to stay here."

"Thank you," Jack said.

"Of course," Fala said. "I will return when, and if, I've heard from Togo."

Maddie

Tardon sat straight up in his high-backed chair, watching the dancing flames in the fireplace beside him. He turned when he heard a knock on the door and called out, "Enter."

The heavy wooden door swung open, and a young man dressed in red robes stepped inside. "Your visitor has arrived, sir."

"Very good," Tardon said without moving. "Please show our guest in."

The young man bowed and exited. Seconds later, he returned with a female Gnome. She wore a white dress and trembled slightly as she came into the room.

Tardon walked over to his guest. He looked at her for several seconds. "Can we get you something, Retta?" he asked.

Retta swallowed hard. "Nnn . . . no, I'm fine."

Tardon addressed the young man. "Thank you. You can leave us now."

The young man bowed again and left, closing the door behind him.

Tardon walked to a small table against a wall that had two chairs at it. He sat and gestured toward the empty chair. "Please, sit with me."

Retta looked around the chamber. It was very simple—just the table and chairs, and a high-backed chair beside the fire, nothing else. She walked slowly to the table, her hands shaking, and sat down across from Tardon.

Tardon forced a smile. "I'd like you to relax, Retta. After all, it was you who requested this meeting."

Retta cleared her throat. "It's just that I was unsure how I would be greeted." She looked down. "Considering recent events."

Tardon nodded. "Ah, yes. You and your father *did* lead your Mountain Gnomes against my Tars—"

"Excuse me," Retta interrupted. "My father was Chief, and I was obligated to follow his orders."

"Very well," he said. "I take it that things have changed?"

"I believe," she began, swallowing hard with each word, "that my father was mistaken to take sides against you. I have seen that Stanton has allowed himself to be led by a boy with no experience, and that is foolish. I cannot, and I will not, allow myself and my fellow Mountain Gnomes to take sides with a fool." Retta paused for a deep breath. "I have come here to offer our services to your cause."

Tardon leaned back. "I must say that this comes as a surprise. I had believed that the Mountain Gnomes were devoted to Stanton and his guard."

"My father was devoted to Stanton," Retta corrected. "I do not intend to repeat his mistakes."

"And what of your fellow Gnomes?" he asked. "Will they support your decision?"

"They already have. We are all ready to join you to build a future with the magical realm at the forefront."

Tardon stood, and Retta quickly did the same. He put an arm around her and guided her toward the door. "Very well, then. We will find a place for you and the rest of the Mountain Gnomes."

"We will serve in any way you deem necessary."

"We will be in touch to let you know what role you will play in our undertaking." He opened the door. "You will hear from us soon."

Retta bowed and left the chamber.

Tardon closed the door and returned to his high-backed chair beside the fire. A small, thin woman in a black robe stepped out of a dark corner. Her hair was steel gray and stood out of her head like tiny wires. She walked behind Tardon and put a thin, bony, stick-like hand on his shoulder and leaned close to Tardon's ear. She whispered hoarsely, "You see, just as I foretold, all the magical creatures are aligning with you."

Tardon patted the old woman's hand. "Yes, Belinda. Just as you said it would be."

"The girl," Belinda said. "Has the aunt gained her trust?"

"She assures me she has."

"Soon, you must go to her—before the boy comes for her."

"And have you seen when that will be?" he asked.

Belinda hissed. "The boy has already returned to the magical realm."

Jack

Jack and The Hawk had fallen asleep, sprawled out beside the fire, its warmth covering them like a thick blanket. Fala entered the small cave and cleared her throat loudly. No one moved. She tried again, and Jack stirred. He opened his eyes, and when he turned over, he saw Fala standing over him. Jack got to his feet quickly and lightly kicked The Hawk.

"I'm sorry, Fala," Jack said. "We both had a long night."

Fala bowed. "That's quite all right."

The Hawk sat up and rubbed his eyes.

"Hello, Allan," Fala said.

"Hello," he replied as he complete his waking stretch.

Jack sat on one of the large rocks by the fire and invited Fala to sit beside him. "Have you been able to get in touch with Togo?"

"Yes," she said. "He will be returning shortly."

"That's great! I can't wait to see him."

"He is most anxious to see you as well. But there is someone else who would like to see you now. I hope you will not be upset that I have taken such a liberty."

Jack looked at The Hawk, who was still trying to wake himself up. Then he looked back at Fala. "I wish you would have said something before," he said. "I don't know if I'm ready to see Benny just yet."

Fala smiled. "Oh, no, young one. I am not *that* brazen." She waved toward the entrance.

A young woman came in. Her long brown hair hung to her shoulders, its red highlights catching the light of the fire. She smiled at Jack, and his heart skipped.

Jack leapt to his feet and ran to her. "Connie! It's so great to see you. How are you?"

"I'm good, Jack. How are you?" Connie asked, hugging Jack. As she pulled away, Jack noticed her look past him and eye The Hawk. "Aren't you Allan Hawkins?" she asked.

The Hawk nodded. "I am. And, who would you be?"

Jack saw the two of them looking at each other and he didn't like it, but he remembered his manners. "Sorry," he said. "Connie, this is my friend, The Hawk."

The Hawk smiled. "It's nice to meet you." He paused. "Wait a minute. Connie? Benny's prized student?"

Jack looked from The Hawk to Connie again. "You two know each other?"

"Only by reputation," The Hawk replied.

"Yes, and you've built quiet a reputation around here." Connie turned away from The Hawk and grabbed Jack's arm. "I need to talk to you. Alone." She didn't wait for Jack to reply; she simply pulled him just outside the cave entrance.

"Jack," Connie said in a voice slightly above a whisper. "I don't know how you got together with Hawkins, but it's not a good idea."

Jack glanced back inside the cave at The Hawk. He shook his head at Connie. "He's on our side."

Connie shook her head. "Don't be so sure about that; his whole family has been devoted followers of Tardon."

"He explained all that. He told me that Tardon wanted him to join the Tars and that he refused. That's why he was in the non-magical realm. He's been hiding from Tardon. He's one of us; I'm sure of it."

Connie sighed. "I hope you're right Jack, but this is something Stanton will want to know about."

Jack's face tightened, and he stared at Connie. "Listen, I'm back, but I'm not here to answer to anyone—not even Stanton."

"I would expect nothing else from you," Connie said. "It doesn't matter; we still need to get to Benny's."

Jack put up his hands. "Hold on; I'm in no hurry to see him."

"What about your parents, Jack? Don't you want to see them?"

He stepped back. "Of course I do, but they haven't exactly been in a hurry to see me."

Connie looked at the ground for a moment, and cleared her throat. "Your mother has been in no condition to go looking for you."

Jack's mouth fell open, and his heart beat like a drum in his chest. "What?! Stanton said that she would be okay."

"Her injuries were worse than we first thought," Connie explained. "And her worrying about you and Maddie has slowed her recovery . . ."

Jack grabbed both of Connie's shoulders, shaking her slightly. "Connie, what is it?"

"She needs to see you. She needs to know that you're okay, or—"

Jack knew what Connie was about to say, and he wouldn't let her speak the words. "Bring me to her, now!"

"Hold on," a familiar voice said. Togo stepped in front of Jack and Connie. "I know that your mother is ill, and Connie can bring her word of your return. But, right now, I believe that your sister needs you more."

Jack couldn't speak. He moved back inside the cave and sat down by the fire.

The Hawk went to Jack's side. "Kid, are you okay?"

Jack nodded but didn't say anything. He watched as Togo and Connie came into the cave. Connie sat beside Jack while Togo greeted his mother, then Togo and Fala joined the others.

Jack addressed Togo. "What's happened to my sister?"

"Physically, she is fine. But, she has put herself under Lisa's influence, and I do not believe that is a safe place."

The Hawk added his opinion. "I told you that Lisa Baxter is no neutral wizard. She is a servant of Tardon's."

"What about you? Who do you serve?" Connie demanded.

The Hawk's eyes narrowed as he looked at Connie. "Just because you've heard about certain members of my family, don't think for a second that you know anything about me, because—believe me—you do not."

Before Connie could retort, Jack took control of the conversation. "If you don't mind . . . Togo." Jack paused when he saw Fala raise an eyebrow at him. "I'm sorry. *Chief* Togo. Please tell me everything you know about Maddie."

Togo nodded. "During the battle, Lisa vanished with your sister. As soon as I was able, I tracked them to Lisa's home far in the west—"

"You tracked them?" Jack interrupted.

"You did want me to keep an eye on your sister, didn't you?"

Jack nodded. "I did, but I never thought that you'd keep it up after the battle."

"Why?" Togo asked. "You never told me not to."

"No, I guess I didn't," he said. "Thank you, Chief. Is there more?"

Togo continued. "I saw your sister, Lisa, and a young witch I do not know leave our realm. They were gone a very long time, but when they returned, they went into the White Mountains, and magical protection prevented me from following. Then, they returned to Lisa's home and are there now. I believe Lisa is trying to turn your sister against us."

Jack didn't move; he wanted to jump up and down and scream his head off, but he remembered Connie's lesson about controlling his emotions.

Finally, Jack let out a slow breath. "Chief Togo, Fala, do you think that Lisa is one of Tardon's followers?"

Togo and his mother looked at each other for a moment, and then Fala nodded to her son.

"It is not our place to say," Togo began. "But, because you ask, I will answer. I cannot say for sure that Lisa is one of the Tars, but we Gnomes are in tune with nature and its forces, and there is something very dark around Lisa. If your sister has put her trust in Lisa, it can be very dangerous."

This time, Jack's emotions got the better of him. He stood up quickly. "Okay, let's go get her!"

The Hawk got up. "Hold on, kid. You can't just go into the western territory, knock on Lisa Baxter's door, and take your sister out of there. That's how you'll get yourself killed."

"Yeah, Jack," Connie agreed. "This is something we have to plan, and something we need to get some others involved in."

Jack chewed his bottom lip and sat back down. "You mean my parents and Benny."

"Yes," Connie said.

Jack looked into the fire for a long few seconds and then stood again. "Okay, let's go to Benny's."

Maddie

Lisa sat at the kitchen table, cradling a hot cup of coffee in her hands. Erin sat across from her, a half-eaten muffin on a plate in front of her.

"I just want you to make an effort," Lisa said. "You don't have to be her best friend."

Erin rolled her eyes. "I don't see why I have to talk to her at all. Unless it has something to do with the cause, I don't really have anything to say to her."

Lisa put the coffee cup down. "It has everything to do with the cause. I need to know that she really believes in what we're doing—that she trusts me."

"I don't see why she's so important," Erin muttered. "Who cares if she's on Stanton's side? We're smarter and stronger than his guard."

Lisa smiled. "I'm glad you realize that, but what you don't realize is that Maddie and her brother are said to have been destined to destroy Tardon, and he puts a great deal of faith in that prediction. He believes that by keeping them apart, it negates their power. Now, if we can convince Maddie to join our side, all the better for us."

"And my being friends with her helps that?"

"I said be *friendly*," Lisa corrected. "You don't need to be her friend, and yes, it helps a great deal."

Erin pushed her plate away. "Fine."

Lisa winked. "Good. Now, go get her for breakfast."

Maddie's eyes opened when a steady stream of sunlight flowed in through the window over the bed. She was still lying in the same position she had started in and wondered how she could have slept so soundly.

She sat up, rubbed her eyes, and stretched, glancing out the window. Somewhere, her parents were probably worrying about her, and Jack was losing his cool. She wanted so badly to see them, to tell them that the things they believed weren't true, that a world run by magic would be a wonderful, peaceful place, and that Stanton and Benny were wrong and the world would not end. She sighed, knowing that Lisa was right. They couldn't just go and tell her parents all of this. Arrangements needed to be made to avoid a battle with Stanton and Benny. Maddie couldn't tell them the truth while they were under Stanton's influence. A knock on the door interrupted her thoughts.

"Maddie," Erin called from the other side of the door. "Are you awake?"

Maddie looked at the door, surprised that Erin was checking on her. "Yes," she answered. "You can come in."

Erin opened the door, a forced smile on her face. "Good morning. Are you hungry?"

Maddie shrugged. "Yeah, I guess I could eat."

Erin sat beside Maddie on the bed. "Is there something wrong?"

Maddie looked down. Did she really want to confide in Erin? Could she trust her with what she was thinking? But, Erin *had* come to see her. Maybe she was trying to be friends, and Maddie thought she could use a friend.

"Well," she said. "I'd really like to see my family."

Erin looked into Maddie's eyes and smiled. "Yeah, I guess you would."

"It's been a while," Maddie went on. "And I miss them." A tear rolled down her cheek   Erin watched her, and could see she was upsetting Maddie. "I'm sorry," she said.

Maddie wiped her face, took a deep breath, and looked back at Erin. "Where's your family?" she asked.

Erin stood up, walked to the window, and looked out into the yard. "I don't know. My parents left me with my grandmother when I was a baby and never came back."

Maddie walked over to Erin and put a hand on her shoulder. "I'm sorry, I didn't mean to upset you."

Erin shrugged. "I never knew them, so I could never miss them the way you miss your family. Besides, my grandmother was very good to me."

"Where is she?"

Erin turned away again. "She died."

"I'm sorry."

Erin didn't answer; she took in several small breaths, and Maddie knew she was crying. Maddie rubbed Erin's back, and Erin wiped her face, taking in one big breath before turning back to Maddie. "You really miss your family, don't you?" she asked.

Maddie nodded, and Erin looked at her for a while. "Okay," Erin finally said. "I'll get a message to them, but you can't tell Lisa."

A smile broke out on Maddie's face and she hugged Erin. But Erin quickly pulled away. "Don't get crazy."

"But what you're doing is so nice."

Erin shook her head. "Yeah, well don't get used to that. I just think it's wrong that you're being kept away from your family, but Lisa doesn't think you're ready to see them."

Maddie's eyes squinted. "But why? I don't understand."

Erin rolled her eyes. "I don't pretend to understand everything Lisa does. I simply accept that her actions are for the good of the cause. I'll send the message right after breakfast."

Maddie held back the urge to hug Erin again. "Thank you," she said. Then she followed Erin to the kitchen.

Jack

"You want to do this right now?" Connie asked.

Jack looked around the room and then refocused on her. "Yes! Right now, if it gets me to Maddie, then let's go now."

Connie didn't argue. "Okay, then. Let's get going."

Jack grabbed his backpack and started for the exit. The Hawk began to follow.

"Wait a second," Connie said, looking at The Hawk. "You can stay here."

Jack looked at Connie, and her face said there was no compromise. But he didn't have time for that. "Maybe you should wait here; I haven't seen my parents in a while and should do this alone." Jack turned to Togo. "Is that all right, Chief?"

Togo bowed. "We will be happy to entertain your friend."

"Thank you," Jack said, and he caught The Hawk's eye again. "I'll be back."

Togo and Fala led Jack and Connie outside the cave and into the forest. A haze was over the forest, dew glistened on the plants, and the sun was still low in the sky. Being in the cave made it hard to keep track of time, but apparently, Jack had slept a day away while waiting for Togo.

Jack bowed to the Gnomes. "Thank you for all that you've done."

"You are most welcome," Togo replied. "Have a safe journey and do not worry about your friend."

"We'll see you very soon," Connie added. "Are you ready, Jack?"

"Let's do it."

Jack followed Connie a few feet away and grasped her hand, the warmth of it making his heart skip a beat. They closed their eyes and vanished.

They appeared in front of a big pine tree that Jack knew to be the passage to Benny's home. Connie let go of Jack's hand and moved toward the tree.

"Wait!" Jack called.

Connie turned back. "What's wrong?"

"I can't go in," he said.

"But you wanted to come here."

"I know. I'm just not ready to see Benny. Please, can you just send my father out?"

Connie looked at Jack. Beads of sweat were forming on his forehead and his whole body trembled. She took his hand.

"Are you all right?"

Jack swallowed hard and cleared his throat. "Yeah, I'm just nervous."

Connie smiled at him. "Don't worry; I'm sure your father will be very happy to see you."

Jack looked down. "I hope so."

Connie said squeezed Jack's hand. "I'm sure of it." She let go and placed her hand on the big pine tree. An opening appeared, and she looked back at Jack. She smiled again and went inside, the opening disappearing behind her.

Jack sat down on the remains of a large tree that had fallen over. He took off his backpack, opened it, and removed a small plastic wallet that contained a dozen Chinese stars. He took out a couple and began throwing them at a tree a few feet away. He threw the stars with precision, each one hitting the tree with a small thud as it was embedded in the bark. When he got up to retrieve the stars and pulled them from the tree, he heard a familiar voice.

"Jack!"

Jack turned and saw his father rushing toward him. His father's tall, thin frame bounded over the fallen tree, and he reached Jack in only a couple of steps. He grabbed Jack and hugged him tightly, as if he would never let go. Jack couldn't help but feel safe within the familiar embrace of his father and hugged him back.

It was long seconds before they broke their welcoming embrace. Jack and Ray took a long look at each other. All his fond feeling for his father washed over Jack and he was glad for the reunion.

Ray mussed Jack's hair. "You need a haircut," he said.

Jack felt his hair. "I guess I do."

Ray put an arm around his son. "Come on. Your mother will be happy to see you."

Jack turned himself loose from his father's arm and took a few steps back. He sat down on the fallen tree again. "I know, and I want to see her," he said. "But I can't go in there."

Ray sat beside Jack and let out a long breath. "Your mother hasn't been well. That's why I didn't come after you."

Jack looked down and nodded. "I understand that. I'm not angry with you; I know she needed you."

Ray squeezed Jack's knee, and Jack knew that his father was pleased that he understood.

Jack continued to look at the ground. "I don't want to see Benny, and I'm pretty sure he won't be welcoming me into his house anytime soon."

Ray nodded. "I understand that you're angry with him, and so does Benny. But he's not one to hold a grudge. He'll be happy you're back—believe me."

Jack looked at his father. "It's more than anger, Dad. I know Benny's your friend, but to me, he's a liar who only looks out for himself."

"That's not true, Jack. It might be how you see it, but Benny's spent a lot of time and energy protecting you and Maddie. He's even put his own life on the line to see that you two were safe—"

"For his own good," Jack interrupted. "He didn't care about us; he cared about what we could do to help him fight Tardon."

"Jack!" Ray scolded. "I'm going to tell you something Benny would never tell you, or even want you to know. When you and your sister were born, Tardon and several of the Tars came for you, determined to kill you. It was Benny who got us all away, and he was tortured nearly to death because he wouldn't tell where you were. It took all of Stanton's guard to rescue him. When you two had to come back, he wanted to protect you, and that's why he didn't tell you about your destiny."

Jack kicked at the dirt. "We still should have been told, and then we could have made our own decision about all of this."

"And what decision would that have been?" Ray asked.

Jack swallowed hard. "I don't want any part of this. I just want my regular life back."

"Then why would you come back?"

"For you, and for Mom . . . and to find Maddie."

"Maddie," Ray whispered.

Jack looked at Ray and his anger quickly took hold. "Yeah! You remember her, don't you? Have you even tried to find her?"

"Just a second, young man. We have people looking for Maddie every minute of the day." Ray paused to take a breath. "There's been no sign of her. We know that Lisa took her from the battle, but we don't know where."

Jack locked eyes with his father. "I have no idea where they were," he said. "But, I can tell you that they are at Lisa's right now."

"How do you know this?" Ray demanded.

Jack wasn't going to tell anyone about the arrangement he'd made with Togo. They had built trust between them, and he wasn't going to betray that—not even to his father.

"It doesn't matter how I know," Jack said. "I just know."

"If she is at Lisa's, we need to make a plan to get her out of there," Ray said.

Jack kicked at the ground again. "It may not be that simple. I don't think Maddie's there against her will, and if she wants to be there, it won't be easy to get her to leave." He paused before making his decision. "I'll see Mom first. Then, I'll go get Maddie."

Ray was glad that Jack was willing to put aside his differences with Benny to see his mother. "Come on then," he said.

Jack hesitated. "Dad, I can't talk to Benny right now."

"Don't worry. I'll take care of it," he reassured him.

They passed through the big pine and into Benny's home. The entrance opened to a living room that led to the kitchen, and a hallway behind that led to two bedrooms. They walked into the living room and Jack looked past it to the kitchen. Benny and Connie were seated at the table, and when he saw Jack, Benny got up and moved his short, stocky frame toward him. Ray stepped forward and met Benny just before he got to the living room.

"He wants to see his mother," Ray said. "I don't think he's ready to talk."

Benny paused for a quick look at Jack, nodded, and returned to the kitchen table.

Jack followed his dad past the kitchen and down a small hallway to a bedroom Jack had once shared with his sister. Ray opened the door slightly and peeked inside. Tina was sitting up in the bed, her auburn hair resting on her shoulders. Her eyes, usually alert and smiling, looked off into the distance, dull and vacant.

"Tina," Ray said gently. Tina slowly turned her head in the direction of his voice.

"There's someone here to see you." He opened the door and waved Jack in.

Jack walked slowly into the room. Tina's eyes opened wide, and the dull glaze brightened.

"Hi, Mom," Jack said. Tina tried to get out of the bed, but he ran to her side. "Don't get up," he said.

Tina wrapped an arm around him and pulled him close. She kissed him on the cheek, and Jack smiled. As tears ran down both her cheeks, she whispered, "I'm so glad you're safe."

"How are you feeling, Mom?" he asked.

"Much better, now that you're here," she replied. Then she looked around the room. "Where's your sister?"

Jack cleared his throat. "She's not here right now, but I'll bring her to see you soon."

Tina smiled at Jack again. "You're a good boy," she said, and fell gently back onto the pillows.

Jack could see that she was exhausted. He kissed her and stood. "You rest, Mom. I'll get Maddie, and we'll both be back soon."

Tina closed her eyes, and Jack and Ray stepped out of the room. Ray closed the door behind them.

"Is she going to be okay?" Jack asked.

"Her injuries have healed. I think the worrying about you and Maddie, along with being hurt, drained her. But, now that she's seen you, I think that will go a long way to getting her healthy."

"I hope so," Jack said. He followed Ray down the hall, past the kitchen, and into the living room.

Ray sat down on the couch. Jack stood with his back to Benny and Connie, who were still sitting at the kitchen table. "How," Ray started, "do you plan on bringing your sister back here?"

"Let me worry about that," Jack said. "I'm leaving now, but I'll be back with Maddie."

Ray stood and assumed a fatherly posture, putting his hands on his hips and speaking in a stern voice. "Just hold on there! You don't get to make decisions like this without me, especially where your sister is concerned."

Jack's first reaction was to push back and argue, but, instead, he took a cleansing breath, and then met Ray's gaze. "Listen, Dad. It's obvious that Mom needs you here, and I think I've proven that I can take care of myself. Besides, I'll have help."

"Connie has told me about your help," Benny interjected, as he walked into the living room with Connie right behind him.

Jack turned around. "Hello, Benny."

"It's good to see you, Jack," Benny said. "But, I understand that you've made a questionable friend."

Jack wanted to be angry, but after being told that Benny was willing to die to protect him, he couldn't find any anger. Yet, he still held his ground. "The last thing I need is a lecture; I know what I'm doing and who I'm doing it with. So, I'll just say goodbye and do what no one else seems to be able to do: find my sister."

Jack headed for the exit, and Ray and Connie followed him. As they came out of the big pine and into the forest, a small, bright ball of light circled them. It landed at their feet and slowly faded to reveal a tiny woman with wings.

"It's a messenger fairy," Connie said.

The fairy bowed and spoke in a tiny voice. "I have a message for Mr. Austin."

Ray stepped forward. "Yes?"

The fairy bowed again. "Your daughter, Maddie, is with Lisa, and she is fine. She misses you very much."

"Where is she?" Ray asked.

The fairy bowed a third time. "I'm sorry," she said. "That is all." She glowed brightly again and shot from the forest.

Ray looked at Jack. "That's it, I'm going to Lisa's right now to get your sister."

"Wait," Jack said. "I think I know how to get Maddie to come to us."

Maddie

Maddie sat at the kitchen table, picking apart a blueberry muffin, but eating little of it. Lisa sat across from Maddie, watching her.

"You should really eat something," Lisa said.

Maddie looked up. "I know. It's just . . ."

Lisa reached across the table and patted Maddie's hand. "I know you miss your family, but we're going to have to be careful when we arrange a reunion."

Maddie had heard all this before. "I know you think that Benny will try to convince me that what I've seen isn't true. I know he won't just let me see my family without trying to get me to stay, but what if we brought my family here?"

"I would love to do that for you," Lisa said. "But after all the influence that Stanton and Benny have had over them, do you think they'd come willingly?"

Maddie dropped what was left of the muffin on the plate. "If I explained things to them, I know they'd see the truth." She stood, walked into the living room, and looked out the window into the front yard. She spotted Erin walking toward the house and their eyes met. Maddie nodded at her, and when Erin returned the nod, she knew the message had been sent.

Erin came into the house, and Lisa rose from her seat. "Where have you been?"

"Just walking," Erin said. "I've seen one of our brothers approaching; he should be here any second."

Lisa waved a hand and the breakfast plates were instantly cleaned and put away. She went into the living room and sat on the couch. "Come, girls," she called. "Let's await our guest."

Maddie and Erin sat in the living room, Erin on the couch beside Lisa, and Maddie on a chair across from them.

Within a few minutes, there was a knock on the door. Lisa immediately got up and gestured for the girls to do the same.

"Please, come in," Lisa said.

When the door opened, a figure dressed in a red-hooded cloak stepped inside. He closed the door behind him and lowered his hood.

The man was tall and thin, and his bald head shined in the sunlight coming in from the window. The skin of his face was dark and tight, and his eyes were set deep within their sockets, giving him a skeletal appearance.

Lisa moved across the living room and extended a hand toward the visitor. "Vance. Welcome to my home. Please, sit down."

Vance looked around the room and sat in a chair beside Maddie's. Lisa, Erin, and Maddie returned to their seats.

"Thank you for the welcome," Vance said. "But, this is not a social call. I bring a message from Tardon." He looked at Maddie. "This message is for *The Destined One*. Tardon wishes to discuss your future. Would that be acceptable?"

Maddie shrugged and Lisa mouthed the word *yes* to her.

"I suppose," Maddie said. "When?"

"Tardon will be here this afternoon," Vance replied. He looked at Lisa. "I'm assuming that will all right with you."

"But of course; I would never refuse a request from Tardon."

Vance stood. "I shall relay your enthusiasm."

Lisa led the way to the front door and held it open for Vance. "Thank you," she said. Vance bowed his head slightly and left.

Lisa watched from the open door as Vance walked away and slowly vanished into the wind. Before she could close the door, a bright light shot from the sky and hovered at the front door. Maddie and Erin came to the door, and when they did, the light landed and slowly faded until a small man with wings stood before them.

"Jingo!" Maddie said.

The fairy bowed. "Miss Maddie, your mother is ill, and your father wishes you to meet him at the home of the Forest Gnomes." Jingo bowed again, glowed brightly, and flew off.

Maddie was speechless. She covered her face with her hands, and her whole body shook.

Lisa put an arm around her. "I'm sorry," she said. "That is unfortunate."

Maddie dropped her hands to her sides and took in several breaths. Tears flowed freely over her face as she looked at her aunt. "Unfortunate? My mother is sick. She didn't drop a carton of eggs on the floor." She walked out into the front yard, and Lisa and Erin followed.

"What are you doing?" Lisa asked.

"I'm going to see my mother."

"Tardon is coming to see you," Lisa reminded. "You can't just leave."

"Watch me!" Maddie said.

Lisa took a step toward Maddie and Erin grabbed her. "You can't stop her," Erin said.

Lisa looked at Maddie and then at Erin. "She can't go," Lisa whispered.

"It's her mother," Erin reasoned. "She has to go. I'll go with her and make sure she's not forced to stay."

With only seconds to make a decision, Lisa nodded. "Okay. I'll explain things to Tardon and if anything happens, you get a message to me right away."

"I will," Erin said before walking into the yard and standing beside Maddie.

Maddie smiled, and the girls joined hands, closed their eyes, and were gone.

Crossed Paths
Part Two

Crossed Paths: Chapter One

Jack, Ray, and Benny appeared in the forest close to the large rock that concealed the entrance to the cave of the Forest Gnomes. Togo was waiting for them, and he greeted them with a smile. "My friends, it's so good to see you." The welcome was for all of them, but Jack knew that the warmth was for Benny.

Benny stepped forward. "It's so good to see you too, Chief." They bowed to each other, and then Benny moved onto business. "Thank you for allowing us, once again, to use your services."

Togo inclined his head toward Benny. "But of course. Myself, and my Gnomes, are at your service, always."

"You do understand that there is a risk involved," Benny said.

Togo smiled. "I wouldn't want it any other way." He posted one of his Gnomes to keep watch and invited the group inside.

Once inside, they made their way to the small cave that Jack had been staying in. The Hawk got to his feet from his seat by the fire and met Jack just inside the entrance. "Everything okay, kid?" he asked.

"Yeah, everything's good," Jack said. "But, that might change very soon." He looked at the group accompanying him. "I'm sorry, everyone. This is my friend, The Hawk."

The Hawk shook hands with Ray and extended his hand to Benny. Benny glanced at The Hawk's hand, but did not take it. Instead, he looked into The Hawk's eyes.

"I know of your family," Benny said. "I hope that their views are not yours."

The Hawk sighed. "It's obvious that you don't know the whole story, but I hope that you will at least give me a chance."

"I tend to give everyone the benefit of the doubt. Some say it is a weakness of mine, but I shall be no different with you."

"That's all I can ask," The Hawk said.

Jack stepped in and explained to The Hawk what was going on. "Here's the situation. We've sent a message to my sister and we're hoping she'll come here. But whether she comes alone is something we'll have to wait and see. Just be ready for anything."

Jack had barely finished his sentence when one of the Forest Gnomes stepped into the cave. "Chief Togo, there are two girls in the forest, just outside the entrance."

"She didn't come alone," Ray said. "Let's go."

The wizards, Togo, and Fala went quickly to the forest, and as they exited the rock opening, Maddie caught sight of Ray.

"Dad!" she yelled, running to him. They hugged, and Ray held her tightly.

"Maddie, it's so good to have you back," he said.

Maddie pulled out of the hug. "Where's Mom?"

"She's at Benny's," Jack answered.

When Maddie saw him, she almost knocked him over with the force of her greeting. She held him tightly, trying to show how much she had missed him.

Jack couldn't help but smile as he looked at his sister. "How are you, sis?"

"Jack, I have so much to tell you, but I want to see Mom first."

"We'll go there soon," he said, looking past his sister. "Who did you bring with you?"

Maddie turned and glanced at Erin, who was standing in the clearing, watching the reunion. "This is Erin. She's . . ."

"Lisa's student," Benny finished. He moved forward to take his turn greeting Maddie.

Maddie smiled at Benny. "Uncle Benny. How are you?"

"I'm well, thank you," he said. "I'm sorry, but I have to ask: how it is that you came to travel with this young lady?"

Erin walked close to the group. "In her time of trouble," she explained, "I thought Maddie could use some support."

Benny bowed his head. "Excuse me for being so forward, but is it possible that you are here only to see that Maddie returns to Lisa?"

Erin took a small breath. "I understand your concern, but I am only here for Maddie."

"Then you will not mind staying here while we take Maddie to see her mother," Benny said.

Erin looked at Maddie. "If that's what she wishes."

"Wait a second," Maddie started to say. But Jack quickly took hold of her arm and pulled her close to him.

"Now's not the time for confrontation," Jack whispered. "I think this will be best—for now."

Maddie raised an eyebrow at Jack. "I just want to see Mom," she said. "I don't care about anything else right now." She turned to Erin. "Let's just do what they want; I need to see my mother."

"That will be fine," Erin said.

Jack walked close to Benny. "The Hawk's coming with us, and that's not a request."

Benny cleared his throat. "Very well. Shall we go?" He walked over to Togo and instructed, "Please, keep an eye on her. And don't take her inside."

Togo nodded his reply and Jack, Ray, Benny, The Hawk, and Maddie all vanished.

Crossed Paths: Chapter Two

The group appeared in the forest clearing just a few feet from the big pine. Benny approached the tree, stopped, and looked at The Hawk before he placed his hand on the big pine. The entrance materialized, and Benny led the way into his home.

Once inside, Benny turned to Ray. "Take Maddie to see Tina," he said. "I have to take care of something."

Ray nodded. "Come on, Maddie. Let's see Mom."

Jack sat down on the couch, and The Hawk sat beside him.

"Aren't you coming, Jack?" Maddie asked.

"I want to give you and Mom some time together," Jack replied. "I'll be in soon."

Maddie shrugged and followed Ray into the small bedroom. Ray knocked on the door and then opened it slowly. His eyes went wide when he looked inside the room. Tina was out of bed, dressed, and just finishing brushing her hair.

"Sweetheart," Ray said. Tina turned to face him. "I guess you're feeling better?"

"I needed to get out of that bed," she said.

Ray crossed the room quickly and took his wife in his arms. "I'm so glad." He kissed her cheek. "I have a surprise for you."

Maddie walked into the room just then. The smile on Tina's face became even wider, and she took a few quick steps toward the entrance to hug Maddie. "Maddie! You've come back to us." She let Maddie go and wiped away the tears flowing down her cheeks.

"Jack said you were sick."

Tina nodded. "I was, but when Jack came back, I started to feel better. And when he promised to bring you to me, I didn't want you to see me in that bed." She hugged Maddie again. "Having my family together once more has made me well."

Maddie smiled. "I'm glad, Mom."

Tina looked around the room. "Where is Jack?"

"He's in the living room," Ray said. "I'll get him."

"No," Tina said. "I'll come out."

Tina, Ray, and Maddie walked into the living room and stopped at the entrance. Stanton was seated with the others. He stood when Tina entered the room, and everyone turned to see what had drawn his attention.

Jack leapt to his feet. "Mom!" he said, hurrying to her side. He kissed her on the cheek and hugged her gently. "You look great. How are you feeling?"

Tina smiled. "Having you and your sister here make me feel wonderful." She looked around the room, nodded at Stanton, and stopped scanning when she reached The Hawk. "I see we have a visitor."

"Yeah," Jack said. "Mom, this is my friend, The Hawk."

The Hawk stood and shook Tina's hand. "You can call me Allan if you like."

Tina stepped back and looked The Hawk over. "I think *The Hawk* suits you for some reason," she said. Then, slowly, her stare faded into a far off thoughtful look. "Wait a second. Allan . . . The Hawk . . . are you . . . Allan Hawkins?"

"Yes, I am."

"Aren't your parents—"

"Followers of Tardon's," The Hawk broke in. "They are, but I do not hold the same views that they do. I am my own person, and I'm here to do what I can to help your son."

Tina walked close to The Hawk and looked into his eyes for an uncomfortably long few seconds. "I believe you," she finally said.

The Hawk smiled. "Thank you."

Tina patted him gently on the cheek and walked over to Stanton. They embraced cordially.

"How are you feeling?" Stanton asked.

"I'm fine. But, why do I think you didn't come here to check on me?"

"I must confess," Stanton said. "That was not my initial reason for coming here today, though I certainly am glad you are feeling better. Benny was kind enough to inform me of your family reunion, and I just couldn't miss out on the warmth of the moment."

Tina shook her head. "I know there's more to it than that, but you can tell me later." She turned toward the couch. "Do any of you mind if I sit with my family?"

Connie and The Hawk quickly left the couch so Tina could sit. She motioned for her children to join her.

Tina put an arm around Maddie and squeezed her gently. "So, Maddie, what have you gotten yourself up to? Where have you been?"

Maddie cleared her throat. "I've been with Aunt Lisa."

Tina's mouth fell open. She swallowed and removed her arm from around Maddie. She turned slightly so that she was facing her daughter. "Well, I can't say that I'm happy about that."

Maddie sighed. "She's been very nice to me. She's shown me that things aren't the way everyone thinks."

Ray leaned forward and asked, "In what way?"

"Oh, Dad," Maddie said. "Aunt Lisa showed me how wonderful the world could be if it was ruled by magic. How peaceful and pollution-free the non-magical realm would become. It's so nice."

Ray looked at Stanton. "So it's true," he said. "My sister has joined Tardon."

Stanton nodded. "I'm afraid it's been that way for a very long time."

Maddie jumped to her feet. "So what?! Tardon and the Tars only want to reverse the damage non-magical people have done to the world. They want to make it the wonderful place it was meant to be, for all creatures of every realm."

The Hawk stepped forward and cleared his throat loudly. "I'm sorry if I'm stepping out of line here, but I have to speak up." He walked in front of Maddie. "I don't know what you've seen or been told, but I know of your Aunt Lisa and her husband, and I know for a fact that they have killed on Tardon's orders. I know that Tardon is a murderer hungry for power, and I know this because Tardon gave orders to Lisa to kill me when I refused to become one of them. You better start recognizing who you can trust. It might save your life."

No one responded; they simply looked at The Hawk, and Maddie gave him a stare that could have burned through lead.

Crossed Paths: Chapter Three

The wind blew Tardon's red robes and whipped his white hair as he walked through the mountain pass with Belinda. Her long, black robes billowed from her frail frame, and she had trouble staying upright as she walked beside Tardon.

"I have seen it," Belinda said. "The girl has returned to her family."

"That is impossible," Tardon said through clenched teeth. "I have sent word of my desire to speak to the girl. Lisa would have stopped her from leaving."

Belinda bowed her head slightly. "Be that as it may, I have seen the girl's desire to return to her family." She stopped walking, as did Tardon. She closed her eyes and the wind picked up, blowing Belinda's wiry gray hair straight back. "I can feel that the powers of the twins are together once more."

Tardon's face was tight as he took in several slow breaths. "If you are right—" he said.

Belinda grabbed his arm, and her eyes flashed red for a moment. "You doubt me after all this time," she said.

Tardon took her hand. "Not now, or ever, have I had any reason to doubt you, but I cannot accept that my loyal servant has allowed such a thing." He let go of her hand. "I must deal with this now." He closed his eyes and vanished from the mountain pass.

Tardon appeared in front of Lisa's house in mid-stride. He kicked open the front door and walked inside.

Lisa heard the door burst open, and she ran to the living room from one of the back bedrooms. She stopped when she saw Tardon, and before she could say anything, Tardon outstretched his arm, causing Lisa to fall to her knees.

Tardon walked close to her, and Lisa fell flat on the floor, writhing in extreme pain. He lowered his hand and the pain ceased. Lisa stayed down. Sweat covered her face, and her chest heaved with each difficult breath.

Tardon knelt beside her and took hold of her hair. He lifted her head while looking into her eyes and speaking very slowly. "Why did you let the girl go?"

Lisa struggled to catch her breath. "She received a message that her mother was ill," she said, panting heavily with each word. "If I tried to keep her here, she never would have trusted me."

Tardon let go of Lisa's hair and walked into the living room.

Lisa took several more breaths and slowly rose to her feet. She staggered into the living room and sat on the couch.

Tardon stood by the window, looking out into the yard. "Where is your student?" he asked.

Lisa took one last deep breath. "She is keeping an eye on Maddie and will make certain that my niece returns."

Tardon turned slowly. He put his hands together as if in prayer and held the tips of his fingers to his chin. He nodded at Lisa. "At least you have done something right," he said. "However, I am curious about something." He walked to the chair across from the couch and sat on its edge, his stare practically drilling a hole into Lisa, making her squirm. "How is it that the girl was able to receive a message from her family when no one was supposed to know where she was?"

A cold sweat beaded up on Lisa's forehead. "I . . . I don't know."

Tardon leaned toward her. "It would appear that someone has given away this information." He reached out and grabbed Lisa's face. "Find out who it was." While pushing Lisa away, he stood to his feet. "I expect to hear from you soon." Tardon then walked out the front door and was gone.

Lisa leaned back on the couch, her heart racing and hands shaking. She knew she would either have to get Tardon the information he wanted, or face his wrath. But she couldn't understand who would have told of Maddie's whereabouts. Only a handful of people even knew where Maddie was, and none of them would have betrayed the secret.

But, Tardon was right. Someone from Maddie's family had known where to send her a message, and the only way that could have happened was if someone had told them where Maddie was. She needed to find out for sure.

She went out into the yard and headed to the bushes in a far corner. "Sasha, can you please come out?" she called softly.

One of the leaves of a bush slowly unfolded, and standing in the middle of the leaf was a small woman with wings. She bowed toward Lisa.

"Did someone ask you to bring a message recently?" Lisa asked.

"Yes," Sasha answered in a tiny voice. "Your student told me you wished to relay a message regarding the girl, Maddie. I was to tell Mr. Ray Austin that she was safe at your home."

Lisa closed her eyes and let out a slow breath.

"Did I do something wrong?" Sasha asked.

"No, of course not," Lisa assured her. "Thank you." She walked slowly back to the house, her stomach feeling uneasy. Everything around her seemed to spin. She leaned against a tree to steady herself. "Oh, Erin," she murmured. "What have you done?"

Crossed Paths: Chapter Four

Maddie yelled at The Hawk. "No! That can't be right. Lisa is kind; she would never hurt anyone."

The Hawk rolled his eyes. "You obviously don't know her well, and I'm sorry you have to find out like this, but what I say is true."

Maddie scanned the room for someone to come to her aid, but she was left to defend herself. She focused on The Hawk. "Why should I listen to you?! I don't even know you."

Jack got up and Maddie felt a wave of relief. At least she could always count on Jack to be on her side.

"Maddie," Jack said. "The Hawk knows what he's talking about. He was forced to leave the magical realm because of Tardon and Lisa."

This was not what Maddie had expected, and she stood silent, shaking her head. No one was listening to her—not even Jack.

Stanton stood, but it wasn't to rescue Maddie. "Maddie, I know that what Allan says is true. His parents are followers of Tardon, but he did refuse to join them, and a sentence of death was placed on his head. Allan fled for his life." He paused and looked at The Hawk. "But only he can tell us the real reason for his return."

The Hawk lowered his head, sighed, and faced the entire group. "I know that some of you already know of my family." He glanced at Connie. "And you may have already made up your minds about me, but you don't know me." He ran his hands through his long hair and swallowed hard. "After the Tars came for me, I went to the non-magical realm and found out quickly that I needed money to survive there. So, I started a magic act and became pretty popular. That's how Jack found me. Being what he is, Jack quickly realized that I wasn't just a guy doing some magic tricks." The Hawk smiled at Jack. "After we spoke, I figured out who he was, and when he talked about coming back here to find his sister and stand up to Tardon, I realized what a coward I'd been and decided to help him . . . whatever the cost may be." The Hawk looked around the room, and it was Ray who offered support in the form of an encouraging nod. The Hawk nodded in reply and went back to his spot, standing in the background.

No one spoke for a few seconds. Then, Jack walked over to Maddie. "Maddie, are you going to join the fight with us?"

She sighed. "Jack, there would be no fight if we could just get everyone to talk. I think this whole thing is just a misunderstanding."

Ray entered the conversation. "Sweetheart, this is much bigger than a simple misunderstanding. Tardon and the Tars want to rule all the realms of existence with magic. This will upset the balance of things and cause the ultimate destruction of all the realms. It's a fact."

"No," Maddie countered. "That's just something you believe because Stanton told you to, but it's not true. Magic can fix what the non-magic has destroyed. Magic can save the world."

Now it was Benny's turn. "The world was created in perfect balance, and the realms were divided to preserve that balance, with none being above any other. To upset the harmony of things would be disastrous. Tardon wants the magical to rule realm. He is threatening the harmony, and the only way he can be stopped is by the power of two in one. You and Jack are destined to save us all."

Maddie gulped. "Me *and* Jack?! But Lisa said *I* was destined to rule over the realms once they were united by magic."

"No," Benny corrected. "The power of two in one is the only power that can save the world: twins—you and Jack—together."

Maddie hung her head. "I don't understand."

"She wasn't there," Jack said, almost to himself.

Benny leaned close to Jack. "What's that, Jack?"

Jack looked at Benny, and the feelings of anger stirred inside of him as he remembered how it was that he found out about his destiny. Jack swallowed those feelings . . . for now. "When Tardon told me about the destiny and the power of two in one, and dared me to try to stop him, Maddie wasn't there. She doesn't know."

"I don't know *what*?"

Jack looked at his sister. "Remember I kept telling you that Benny was keeping something from us?" He glanced at Benny and then went on. "He was, and when Tardon thought he had us beat, he told me that when we were born, it fulfilled an ancient saying that the power of two in one would save the world. We're the only twins in the magical realm; we have the power of two in one, but Tardon doesn't think we can beat him. I know, though, that we can. Together." Jack stopped talking and looked at Maddie for a few seconds. "Help me, Maddie. Please."

Maddie shook her head. "Why should I believe you? You wanted nothing to do with this from the very beginning, and now you want to save the world."

Jack stepped even closer to Maddie and put his hands on her shoulders. "You're right. I didn't want anything to do with magic, and I'm still not crazy about it, but Tardon tried to kill Mom, and now he's trying to take you away from us. I can't let that happen."

His eyes filled with tears. "I found out what it's like to be without my family, and I don't want us to be separated ever again."

"But the things I've seen . . . the world can be a beautiful place if it's run by magic."

"Maddie," Tina chimed in. "The world is already a beautiful place, and it is based on a harmony of existence that Tardon will destroy if we allow him to."

Stanton interjected. "Maddie, since you were shown their side of things, please permit me to show you something." He sat on the couch and motioned for her to sit beside him. He held out both hands, and a glass ball appeared between them, beginning to spin slowly. "This globe contains a memory of the last conversation I had with Tardon, right after you were born. It was my final attempt at convincing him to give up his plans."

Maddie looked closely at the ball and what looked like a TV show began to form inside of it. It showed Stanton face to face with Tardon, and Tardon was speaking.

"You can hide *The Destined Ones* for now, but you know that I will find them and destroy them." Tardon walked very close to Stanton. "And, after I have won, I will number you among the many slaves of my empire. Like all the creatures of all the realms, you will kneel before me."

"How you dream," Stanton answered. "I will die stopping you, if need be."

Tardon laughed. "Eventually, I will see to that myself."

The image in the globe then faded to black, and the globe vanished. Maddie leaned back and held her hand to her mouth. Stanton put an arm around her.

"I want you to think about something," he said. "Even if the world could become the beautiful place they have shown you, is it worth the price of all creatures being enslaved and made subservient to Tardon? I believe that is too high a price to pay for anything."

Maddie realized that Stanton was right. No one would go to so much trouble to overtake a realm without being in full control of it. Her eyes filled with overflowing tears. She turned to her mother. "Mom, how could I be so foolish?"

Tina hugged Maddie. "Oh, honey, you're not the first one to be taken in by a smooth talker."

"I should say not," Stanton interjected. "Tardon has a great many followers and, so far," he paused to acknowledge The Hawk, then turned back to Maddie, "only two have been smart enough to see through his blindfold of lies."

Maddie's body shook as she cried, and Tina held her close. "It's all right; you're back with us now," her mother cooed.

Maddie took a deep breath and wiped her face. "What about Lisa and Erin? Maybe they'd change if they knew the truth."

Ray sighed. "I can't see that happening. My sister has been so corrupted by Tardon and her husband that I don't think she could recognize the truth."

"Can we try?" Maddie pleaded. "She is part of our family."

Before Ray could answer, Jack interrupted. "Dad, can I talk to you for a minute? *Outside*?"

Ray shrugged and got up. Jack looked at Stanton and Benny. "Can you two come with us?"

Stanton and Benny exchanged glances and then followed Jack outside. They stepped out into the forest that was now being warmed by the late afternoon sun.

"Okay, Jack," Ray said. "What's on your mind?"

"Well," he said, looking at Stanton and Benny. "I need your opinion on this. What if we do what Maddie wants and try to convince Lisa to join us?"

"That's useless!" Ray yelled. "My sister will never come back; she's bought into everything Tardon has told her."

"I believe you on that, Dad, but if we let Maddie go back to Lisa, she can lead us to Tardon and maybe expose a weak spot."

Benny scratched his head. "There could be something to that."

Ray exploded. "You're talking about putting Maddie's life in jeopardy, and I'm not going to let that happen!"

"I believe we can keep her safe," Stanton said.

Ray looked at Stanton, and something in his gaze calmed Ray. "You think this is a good idea?"

"I think that any way we can gain insight into Tardon's plans only helps us to stop him," Stanton explained.

Jack put a hand on his father's shoulder. "Dad, this is bigger than just us."

"Do you really believe that?"

Jack lowered his hand and looked away for a second. "I didn't at first, but now I do."

Ray patted Jack's back. "Okay, but let's try to get Lisa to come for Maddie—that way, we're in control."

"That," Stanton said, "sounds like a plan."

Crossed Paths: Chapter Five

Lisa sat on the couch in her living room. Her chest felt heavy and her body trembled like a rabbit being cornered by a wolf. *How could this have happened?* She wondered. Erin didn't even like Maddie. Why would she have helped her like this?

Lisa stood and began to walk slowly around the couch. She wondered if she'd done something wrong. Was she not a good teacher? Did she not make the goals of the cause clear? Had she upset Erin in some way? Was this Erin's way of getting rid of Maddie? She had been unhappy with Maddie being brought into the group, and Erin never really had understood the importance of keeping Maddie close, but Lisa had just chalked that up to Erin's inexperience.

Lisa had always thought that, in time, Erin would understand. But, maybe that was just another shortcoming on Lisa's part. She certainly thought that she knew Erin. After all, she had been Erin's only family figure for nearly a year. She had welcomed Erin into her home, helped her to hone her considerable magical skills, and taught her what it would mean for all the realms to be ruled by magic. She had treated Erin like a daughter, and now, Lisa felt betrayed. She suddenly stopped walking.

How deep did this betrayal go? Lisa wondered. Had Erin changed sides? *Could it be possible?* If she had, Erin certainly did put on a convincing performance when showing her disdain for Maddie.

Lisa shook her head and began to circle the couch again. She knew what had to be done. This had to be brought to Tardon's attention. At the very least, Erin had given away Maddie's location, and at the very worst, she had turned traitor. Either way, Erin's actions could not go unaddressed. Lisa took a deep breath, walked outside, and faded into the wind.

Lisa's feet kicked up the loose gravel of the mountain pass as she appeared out of nothing in the White Mountains. She took a few steps toward the solid rock of the mountainside and put her hand out in front of her. The rock wall opened to reveal a small pathway that led to a dark cave. The path disappeared behind her as she stepped into the mouth of the cave where the two young men who had led Lisa, Erin, and Maddie into the lounge on their last visit greeted her. They both bowed their heads as Lisa appeared.

"Please let Tardon know that I wish to see him," Lisa said.

"Right away, Miss Lisa," one of the guards replied. He tapped the side of the cave, and a ball of light shot down the pathway away from Lisa and the two guards.

It was only seconds before the ball of light returned, and the guard who sent it bowed again. "Follow me," he said. He led Lisa down the pathway to the large wooden door of Tardon's chamber. The guard knocked twice, and Tardon answered from the other side.

"Enter!"

The guard opened the door. "Miss Lisa is here," he said.

Lisa heard Tardon answer, "Bring her in."

The guard pointed the way, and Lisa went in, closing the door behind her.

"So," Tardon said from his seat beside the fire. "I assume you have gotten to the bottom of the mystery."

Lisa bowed her head slightly. "Yes. It was my student, Erin, who sent the message that alerted Maddie's family to her whereabouts."

Tardon leaned back in his chair, tilted his head upwards, and closed his eyes. He let out a long breath before looking back at Lisa. "I suspected as much. What do you think we should do about this?"

Lisa didn't hesitate. "I know the penalty for such a betrayal."

Tardon stood and gripped Lisa's shoulder. "Very well. I have already made the necessary arrangements." He called to the guard who was waiting just outside his door. "Bring in our guest."

The door opened, and a small figure entered the chamber—Retta. Tardon greeted her at the door. "Are you ready for your first task in the name of our cause?"

"Yes," she said. "What is your wish?"

Tardon looked at Lisa and then at Retta. "It seems that one of our young recruits has betrayed us; I have been told that she is with the Forest Gnomes."

Lisa looked at Tardon. How could he know where Erin was? She didn't dare ask, however.

Tardon continued. "I need you to pay a visit to your forest cousins. Find our young, wayward friend, and as soon as the opportunity presents itself, kill her."

Crossed Paths: Chapter Six

Tardon had one of his guards transport Retta into the Gnome's Forest. The idea was to make it appear that she had traveled a great distance. In reality, she only had to walk a short way to the large rock that marked the entrance to the Gnome cave. As she moved through the trees and closer to the clearing, Retta heard the voices of three gnomes, two of which she recognized as belonging to Togo and his mother, Fala. Retta took a deep breath and stepped into the clearing.

The Gnome with Togo and Fala moved quickly to block Retta's path. "Who are you, and what is your business here?" he demanded.

Togo and Fala had risen from where they sat on the ground beside a young girl Retta did not know. She presumed her to be the one Tardon had sent for.

"I am Retta, Chief of the Mountain Gnomes," she said. "I have come to see Chief Togo."

Togo had walked behind his guard. "Let her pass," he commanded.

The guard stepped away, and Togo greeted Retta. "Retta, it is so good to see you," he said as they embraced.

"Yes," Fala said from just behind Togo. "How are things with our mountain cousins?"

"As well as can be expected," she answered.

Togo invited Retta to sit with them before returning to his seat beside the girl Retta did not recognize. Fala and Retta sat on either side of them, while the guard continued to keep watch.

Retta looked at the girl and then at Togo. "Who is your young guest?" she inquired.

"She is a companion of our Miss Maddie, and a student of Lisa's," Fala answered. She then addressed Erin. "This is Chief Retta of the Mountain Gnomes."

Erin recognized that Retta was someone of importance, and she stood to give a small bow. "It is very nice to meet you."

Retta had also stood. "And you as well," she said.

Before they could return to their seats, Jack, Maddie, and the rest of the wizards appeared in the clearing. Togo and Fala rose quickly at the appearance of their friends.

"It's so nice to have you back," Togo greeted.

Stanton returned the greeting. "It's nice to see you also." He turned to Fala. "And the lovely Fala. How are you?"

"I am fine," she replied. Then she faced Benny and spoke softly. "We have kept an eye on the young one as you asked. Not a very glamorous job, I must say."

Benny smiled. "No I would think not, but it was an important one, and we thank you."

Maddie saw Erin and began to walk towards her, but Connie put an arm out in front of her, and Maddie stopped. "Maddie," Connie warned. "Greet your friend, but don't say anything about what we've discussed."

Maddie looked over Connie's shoulder to where Erin sat. "Okay, I get it."

Connie lowered her arm and Maddie went over to Erin.

Jack watched Maddie say hello to Erin as he assessed things. He leaned close to Stanton. "How come no one's mentioned the fact that Retta is here, and why do I have the feeling she is here for a reason?"

Stanton patted Jack's back. "Yes, she is. You don't think we've been sitting around, just waiting for you and your sister all this time?"

"Then how about filling me in on what's been going on?" Jack asked.

"Why not," Stanton said with a grin. "Come with me." They walked over to Retta, said their hellos, and then Stanton suggested the three of them take a walk.

They didn't go far before Stanton began by addressing Retta. "I take it you've been successful."

"Yes," Retta replied. "But, Tardon's quick acceptance of my proposal has made me think he is not entirely convinced."

"I would expect his skepticism, and I would expect him to test you."

"He has given me a task," Retta informed him. "It seems that Tardon and Lisa suspect her student of betrayal. I have been sent to punish her."

Jack had been listening intently. "Just a second," he said to Stanton. "Tell me if I got this right. You've asked Retta to go to Tardon and convince him that she wants to join him, and now he has asked her to punish Erin to prove herself."

Stanton seemed impressed. "You have caught on quite quickly, but you should know that Tardon doesn't simply punish those he believes to have acted against him . . ."

"I know," Jack said. "I figured he wanted Retta to kill Erin." He looked back toward the clearing and rubbed the back of his head. "You know, this could help us—"

"Convince Erin to join our side?" Stanton finished for Jack. "I thought the same thing. Come, let's see if we are right."

"Just a second," Retta said. "Are you suggesting I give myself away to someone so close to Tardon—and so conniving?"

Stanton's dark eyes showed understanding for Retta's concern. "My dear Retta. I assure you, once the young lady hears why you came here, she will not be returning to Lisa." He put a hand on her shoulder. "Even if I have to take matters into my own hands."

In spite of her reluctance, Retta nodded her understanding.

"Come," Stanton said. "Let's see what the young Miss Erin's reaction will be."

When Jack, Stanton, and Erin returned to the clearing, everyone was sitting on logs, rocks, and the ground, engaged in various conversations. If there had been a fire going, one would assume this was a friendly camping trip . . . except where Erin was concerned. She sat away from the group with Maddie beside her, but she was not part of the conversation. She sat on the end of the dead log, staring straight ahead.

Jack headed to his sister and sat beside her, while Retta took a seat with Togo and Fala.

Stanton stood before the group. "Excuse me, we have an important matter to discuss."

Erin got up and cleared her throat. "If that's the case, then Maddie and I should be leaving."

"I don't think so," Stanton corrected her. "You see, the important matter concerns *you*."

Crossed Paths: Chapter Seven

Lisa walked through the tall grass toward the small, decrepit farmhouse. The roof had faded from years of being beaten by the sun, the shutters barely hung on the widows, and the entire exterior cried for a coat of paint. She stepped onto the creaky porch and knocked twice on the splintered wooden door. After waiting five seconds, she knocked twice again. The door opened and a short, muscular man appeared and motioned for her to come in. He leaned his head out the door and took a quick look around before going inside and closing it behind him.

Lisa stood just inside the entrance, surprised that the interior was so nice. Instead of being broken down and in need of care, the small home was neat, clean, and quite comfortable looking. The house was tiny—just a living room and a kitchen—but it was quite luxurious compared to its exterior.

"Come sit." Gavin beckoned to his guest as he stepped into the living room and sat in a leather armchair.

Lisa sat in an identical chair just beside Gavin. "You really need to do something about the outside of your house," she informed him.

"Yeah," he retorted. "At least it keeps Tardon's people away . . . most of them," he added.

Lisa ignored the comment. "I need your help."

Gavin leaned forward. "The last time I helped you, I made a few people angry. What is it this time?"

Lisa closed her eyes and took a short breath before opening them again. "Tardon has placed a death sentence on Erin's head and has sent someone to carry it out. I need you to stop it and get Erin someplace safe."

Gavin rubbed his face and then ran his hands through his black, curly hair. "Where is she?"

"She's escorted Maddie to visit her family, but is supposed to bring her back to my house."

"You realize that Ray and Tina are never going to let that happen. They'll do everything they can to keep Maddie with them," he said.

Lisa didn't want to inform Gavin of all that had happened since she had taken Maddie from the battle, so she stayed on the current topic. "Will you do this?" she begged.

"Of course. I'm not going to let Tardon take a young life if I can help it. Who has he sent?"

Lisa hesitated for a moment. "Retta."

Gavin sat straight up. "Of the Mountain Gnomes," he gasped. "Don't tell me she's joined Tardon."

"It appears that she has," she replied. "But can we please focus on one matter at a time?"

"Fine. Do you know where they went?"

"I could assume one of two places."

"Benny's or with the Forest Gnomes," Gavin answered before Lisa could. "I will go to the Forest Gnomes first. It seems to be the most likely place where they could stay out of sight. Now, I have a question for you. Have you had a change of heart and seen the danger of Tardon's plan?"

"I don't know." Lisa sighed. "Just save Erin, please."

"I will," Gavin assured her. "I will send you a message when I have her safely hidden."

After Gavin agreed to take on the task of saving Erin's life, Lisa left him. Having spent so much time in the company of both sides, Gavin couldn't believe that the Mountain Gnomes had gone over to Tardon—not after all they'd done to help fight against him. And after Retta's father had died fighting the Tars, it seemed highly unlikely. To Gavin, it seemed something that Stanton would have arranged. Yes, he thought, that made much more sense, but just in case, it seemed best to send Benny a message to let him know about the plan to kill Lisa's student.

Gavin opened his front door, but before he could summon the messenger fairy, he was hit hard in the chest by a blast of hot air and staggered backwards into the house. Two men in red cloaks followed him inside. He took two short breaths and put up a hand to defend himself, but was hit with another blast of hot air that knocked him to the ground.

One of the intruders stepped close, grabbed Gavin by the shirt, lifted him, and tossed him into the armchair. "Now," the man said. "We're not here to hurt you; we just want to know why Lisa was here."

Gavin took in a few more breaths. "Just to say hello," he gasped.

The intruders exchanged glances. "We're not here to play games," the first man said.

"That's too bad," Gavin answered. "I thought we might play hide and seek."

The second intruder took a step toward Gavin. "You're not funny."

"Maybe not," he said. "But I am gone." And, just like that, he disappeared.

Crossed Paths: Chapter Eight

Gavin appeared in the yard of Lisa's house just as she approached the front door.

"Gavin," Lisa said, surprised to see him. She took in his frazzled state. "What's wrong?"

Gavin checked his surroundings and spoke very quickly. "Two of Tardon's men came to my house seconds after you left. They were looking for you, and I don't think it was for anything good."

"What did they say?"

"They wanted to know why you came to see me. I suspect they know you're trying to save your student."

Lisa held her hand over her mouth. "That would mean—"

"That they're planning on killing you as well," Gavin said bluntly.

Lisa stumbled backwards and rested against the house. "That's impossible. I've done everything Tardon has ever asked of me. How could . . ."

Gavin walked within inches of Lisa and studied her for a moment. "Tardon doesn't care about you, or anyone else. I've told you before—he doesn't want a co-ruler; he wants servants and slaves, and to be in complete control of all the realms. It's time you realized that Stanton is right: if Tardon succeeds, it will mean the end of the world."

Lisa didn't say anything. She simply kept shaking her head, not wanting to believe what Gavin was saying, but still knowing that something was not right.

Out of nowhere, five red-cloaked people appeared in Lisa's yard. Gavin reacted quickly. He waved a hand and sent a large rock flying toward one of them, hitting him in the head and knocking him to the ground. One of the Tars responded by holding both hands up, and Gavin was lifted high into the air. When the Tar put his hands down, Gavin crashed hard into Lisa's flower garden.

Lisa quickly came out of her shock and ducked out of the way of a bright orange ball that had been sent in her direction. It hit the house and exploded where she had been a second before. She realized that Gavin's speculation had been correct and that her life was in danger. She straightened up, raised both arms over her head, and clapped her hands together. A large gray cloud appeared over the yard, and the wind swirled violently, but only affected the Tars. They couldn't move, held in place by the wind that encircled them. It spun faster and faster around them, making the circle tighter with each rotation. The wind squeezed the Tars tightly together, and with a loud *POP!*, the wind and the Tars were gone.

Gavin dusted himself off and limped to the front steps of the house where Lisa was. Her face was soaked with sweat and she shook with both anger and fear. Gavin helped her to sit on the steps.

"I don't believe it," she gasped. "He really wants to kill me."

"It appears that way," Gavin said.

Lisa took a long breath in an attempt to settle herself. "Well, if he wants me dead, then he'd better come for me himself."

"Hopefully we can avoid that. The question is: what do you want to do now?"

Lisa glared at Gavin. "I can't possibly go to Stanton and expect him to welcome me with open arms."

"No," he agreed. "But maybe you can start with trying to repair your relationship with Ray."

"Maybe I can at least offer him an apology," she speculated.

"That would be a good way to start."

"But we still have to stop Retta from killing Erin."

"I don't think you'll have to worry about that. Something tells me Retta hasn't really gone over to the Tars."

"Well," Lisa said. "We need to find out for sure."

Crossed Paths: Chapter Nine

Erin looked at Stanton and tried to be respectful. "Excuse me, but I don't know how anything you have to discuss would have anything to do with me."

Stanton inclined his head toward her. "Believe me, it does, and it is very important. So, please. Let me explain."

Erin sat down again and her leg shook as Stanton began.

"For the past month, our friend Retta has been doing her best to convince Tardon that she wishes to join him, and now, to test her devotion, he has given her a task."

Erin's impatience took hold. "How does this concern me?"

"Her task is to kill you," Stanton stated bluntly. His words had the desired effect.

Erin jumped up and defended herself. "I don't believe it!" she yelled. "You just want me to leave Maddie here."

"Of course we want Maddie here," Tina interjected as Retta got to her feet.

"If I may," Retta said, then addressed Erin. "It seems that Tardon was upset by the fact that Maddie's family was able to get a message to her, and it was Lisa who discovered that you had sent them a message that gave away Maddie's whereabouts. Tardon considers that action a betrayal, and with Lisa's consent, he has sent me to carry out your death sentence."

Erin continued to look at everyone's face, especially Maddie's, in a desperate hunt for some sign that this wasn't true. "I don't believe it! Lisa would never let that happen. It's just not true."

"It is true," Lisa said as she and Gavin stepped out of the thick of the trees and into the clearing.

Ray and Tina were up quickly and moved in front of Maddie. Benny positioned himself beside Stanton, and Connie stepped behind Erin. The Hawk took Jack's lead and went to the front with him.

"What are *you* doing here?" Jack demanded.

Ray looked at Tina, and she put an arm around Maddie as Ray stepped in beside Jack.

"You have some nerve showing up," Ray said.

Lisa lowered her head, unable to look her brother in the eye. "I know."

Gavin came to Lisa's aid. "She has something to say." He surveyed the group before him. "To all of you."

"Stop acting as her protector," Benny ordered. "I was foolish enough to allow you to bring her into our midst once before; I will not be so foolish a second time."

Gavin's plea then went to Stanton. "Just hear her out," he begged.

Lisa swallowed hard and addressed the small assembly. "I put you in a terrible situation and I'm sorry. I've made mistakes and I've listened to the false promises of the wrong people for too long." Her eyes met Erin's. "And I've put your life in peril, but I promise I will keep you safe, even at the cost of my own life." She lowered her head and when she looked up, she was eye to eye with Ray. "Ray, I'm so sorry. I turned my back on you, and I tried to convince your daughter to do the same. I was wrong." She got down on her knees in front of Ray and bowed her head. "I pledge my allegiance to you, and vow to protect your family."

Ray looked to Tina, who was holding Maddie tight and had no advice to give.

"Get up, Lisa," Ray said. "I want to believe you, but how can I? How can any of us ever trust you?"

Stanton spoke up. "There is a way to know her heart." He found Connie and waved her forward.

Connie walked slowly toward Stanton who stood by while he helped Lisa to her feet. "Lisa," he said. "Please, sit over here." He pointed to a log lying close by, and then turned to Connie. "Please, Constance, tell us Lisa's true feelings."

Connie hesitated. This was a power she truly despised having. The ability to look inside a person—to know their innermost feelings—was an intrusion of a personal privacy. However, Connie knew that Lisa could not simply be allowed to join them based on her words. Connie sat down beside Lisa and closed her eyes.

A light blue mist rose slowly from the top of Connie's head, moved slowly toward Lisa, hovered for a moment, and went *into* Lisa's chest. For several seconds, Connie shook, and after a moment, the mist left Lisa and returned to Connie. She fell backward, and Jack caught her just before she hit the ground.

"Connie, are you okay?" Jack asked as he guided her into a sitting position.

Connie didn't answer. Sweat dripped from her every pore, and she was breathing as if she'd just run ten miles. It took a few minutes for her to compose herself, but when she did, she looked at Ray. "Your sister's heart is true."

Erin stood and went to a side of the clearing by herself. Maddie saw her and followed.

"Erin," Maddie said. "What's wrong?"

"I don't know where I belong," Erin said through tear filled eyes.

"You belong here," Maddie assured her as she put an arm around Erin.

"I don't know. How can I just turn my back on what I was taught to believe?"

"Because what you believed wasn't true," The Hawk answered as he walked toward the girls.

"How can I just fight against him now?" Erin asked.

"The same way I can," The Hawk said. "Remember that Tardon tried to kill you, and by fighting him, we stop him from killing others."

"You were never really one of them," Maddie added. "You took a big risk to let my family know that I was safe. You wouldn't have done that if your heart had truly been with them. You know, and you've probably always known, that they're liars and murderers and have to be stopped."

Erin didn't say anything, and The Hawk stepped in front of her. "They wanted you dead," he reminded her. "That should make you angry."

"It does," Erin admitted.

"Use that," The Hawk instructed. "Let that be your fuel to fight against them."

Erin thought about The Hawk's words. She did feel anger—a deep anger—and an anger that needed satisfaction. She could, and she would, fight to satisfy it.

Jack heard the conversation Maddie had with Erin and he heard The Hawk do his part to convince Erin to join them, but he still felt an uneasiness about it all. He saw Connie read Lisa's emotions and still wasn't convinced. When he noticed that Tina stayed in the background, he thought he knew why. He went over to his mother and sat down on a large rock beside her.

"Hey, Mom," Jack said. "How are you feeling?"

Tina smiled at him. "Good, Jack. How are you?"

He looked down. "I get the feeling you know."

"I get the feeling you came over for more than just to see how I am."

"What do you think about Lisa's change?" he asked.

"It's no secret that Lisa and I were never the best of friends, but Connie's told us that her intentions are sincere."

"And you believe that?"

"The magic that Connie used cannot be fooled—of that there is no doubt. Whether or not those feelings change, we'll have to wait and see." Tina patted Jack's leg. "Don't worry," she assured him. "I'll be keeping an eye on her."

"What about her?" Jack said, indicating Erin with a head tilt.

"She's Lisa's student," she said. "I think she'll follow whatever Lisa does, but . . ."

"It wouldn't hurt to keep an eye on her," he finished.

"No, it wouldn't." Tina laughed.

Jack got up, kissed his mother on the cheek, and headed straight to Maddie. He took her by the hand and led her to the edge of the forest, away from everyone else.

"What's up?" Maddie asked.

"I missed you," Jack answered. "I wanted to know that you're okay."

"I am," she said. "I understand things now, but I feel kind of foolish that I was so easily taken in. I really wanted everything they showed me to be real. I want the world to be a wonderful place for everyone."

"You know, sis . . . I think that's up to us."

Maddie stepped back in feigned surprise. "Is that *you* talking?"

Jack laughed. "I know, I didn't want anything to do with this, but the more I learn about Tardon, the more I believe that it's up to us to stop him." He paused and looked into her eyes. "I need to know that you'll be with me through it all."

She folded her arms. "Do you doubt me?"

"I said that wrong," Jack quickly corrected himself. He took a small breath. "I'm making you a promise. I promise to do all I can to fulfill our destiny, no matter what. Will you make the same promise?"

Maddie's eyes filled with tears. "Yes, I promise to do all I can to fulfill our destiny, no matter what."

They embraced and then went back to the clearing.

Paths United
Part Three

Paths United: Chapter One

When Jack and Maddie returned to the clearing, Ray and Tina were waiting for them.

"Are you two okay?" Ray asked.

"Yeah, we're good," Jack answered.

Tina beamed and stepped between the twins, putting an arm around each of them. "It's so nice to have our family back together."

"It sure is," Ray agreed.

It was then that Jack noticed none of the Gnomes were present. "Where are Togo and Fala?"

"They suggested an open air feast and are making the preparations. Stanton and Benny thought it would be a good idea to place a cloaking spell over the clearing . . ." Ray's voice trailed.

"In case Tardon comes looking for Lisa," Maddie said, finishing for him.

"Exactly," Tina answered.

The family moved into the clearing and took a seat on a log. The sun was beginning to set, and Connie lit a small fire in the center of the clearing. The image of a camping trip was complete just in time as several of the Gnomes, led by Togo, Fala, and Retta came out of the cave entrance, carrying baskets filled with breads, fruits, berries, and nuts of all kinds.

Since everyone was already sitting in a circle around the fire, the Gnomes placed the baskets on the inside of it beside the logs and rocks being used as seats. Togo stepped into the center of the circle and spoke.

"Today our friends have found their families again and a healing has begun. We give thanks to our Great Mother Nature." Everyone bowed their heads for a moment and raised them again when Togo raised his. "Now, let's eat!"

As they feasted, Benny joined the Austin family and sat beside Ray. "How are you doing?" he asked.

Ray gave Benny a sideways glance. "I'm fine."

"That's good," he said. "How do you feel about Lisa joining us?"

Ray put down the roll he was gnawing on. "If you and Stanton want her on our side, that's a decision I'll leave to you. As far as welcoming her back to my family, tell her not to hold her breath."

"She *did* make a solemn vow," Benny pointed out.

"Don't you think she made that same vow to Tardon?" Ray inquired. "You know the saying: actions speak louder than words, so let's just wait and see."

"I think that's a logical approach," Stanton added, as he joined the small gathering. "We have more pressing matters to discuss at the moment." He took a seat on a large boulder.

"Agreed," Benny said. "Tardon will be looking for Lisa."

"I'm sure he already has someone on that," Stanton agreed. "And, it is essential that we allow him to believe his initial plan has worked."

"Erin," Maddie whispered.

Stanton patted Maddie's shoulder. "Yes. Erin. I believe it best if we hide her and allow Tardon to believe that the death sentence has been carried out."

"What about Lisa?" Tina asked. "If Tardon is looking for her, how do we keep her from being found?"

"I've considered that," Stanton replied. "I think we should hide her with Erin for the time being."

"That's fine," Ray said. "But how do we get to Tardon?"

"I've been thinking about that," Maddie offered. "Lisa followed Tardon, and now she's joined us—"

"So she says," Ray interrupted.

"Yeah," Jack agreed. "So she says."

"That's not the point I'm trying to make," Maddie said.

"What is your point?" Tina asked.

Maddie looked at Stanton. "We have a lot of people on our side, right?"

Stanton nodded. "The numbers of the guard are impressive, as are those on our side who are not members of the guard."

"They have families, right?" Maddie pressed.

"Of course."

"Are some of their family members followers of Tardon's?"

Stanton's eyes began to widen as he started to recognize what Maddie was indicating. "I'm certain some of them are."

"Wait a second," Tina interjected, as she too saw where Maddie was headed. "You're not suggesting that we have people go to known Tars to try to talk them into joining us?"

"I am," Maddie replied.

"Why not?" Jack said. "I think it's a good idea; maybe they don't know the whole story . . . maybe they believe the wrong things."

"The Tars are very dangerous people who will do anything to aid Tardon. We can't put people in jeopardy," Ray reminded everyone.

"I think they'd be in less danger from their own families, and some of them might not be as devoted to Tardon as we think," Maddie suggested.

"There's something to that," Benny said. "I've long thought that several of the Tars only stayed out of fear. If we offered them an option, perhaps they would welcome the opportunity to join us."

"I believe you're right, Benjamin," Stanton said. "I'm certain some of Tardon's followers are not acting entirely of their own will, but how to begin—that's the question."

"How about we assemble our allies and ask them to go to their friends and the families of those that are neutral? Then we can move onto those who are known Tars," Maddie said.

"It would be safer to begin with neutral parties," Ray said.

Stanton rose. "I will assemble the guard. Benjamin, bring everyone to the compound tomorrow, and ask Togo to provide lodging within the safest of caves." He then looked at Maddie. "Well done, Maddie," he said before he bid them all farewell, disappearing to make the preparations.

Paths United: Chapter Two

Togo and Fala led the wizards and Retta down deep into the caves of the Forest Gnomes, settling them all in a large cave. The Gnomes had placed about thin mattresses for the wizards to sleep on, and had lit a fire in a large pit at the center to take off the chill. Fala and Togo wished them all a good night and then escorted Retta to a sleeping quarter of her own—something more suitable for the Chief of the Mountain Gnomes.

The wizards chose sleeping spots. Ray and Tina were beside each other, Erin and Lisa were in a corner of their own, and Jack and Maddie were grouped with The Hawk and Connie close to the fire. Benny moved his mattress close to the entrance and sat up, overseeing the group, and by the looks of it, not intending to sleep.

Jack also sat up watching the group, especially Lisa. She and Erin were lying down, but they were speaking to each other very quietly.

"Connie," Jack whispered, and she moved silently next to Jack.

"What is it?"

Jack kept watching Lisa as he spoke to Connie. "What you did with Lisa . . ."

"Read her feelings," Connie said.

"What is that, exactly?"

"It's not a very common power," Connie began. "It's kind of a lie detector. Not that I can tell if someone's telling the truth, but I can feel what their emotions are. And by that, I can tell if someone's words are sincere." She sighed. "To be honest, it's not something I like to do. Feelings are very personal things, and I think it's sort of an intrusion on someone's privacy. So, I don't use that power very often."

"Can someone's feelings be misread?" Jack asked.

Connie smirked. "You want to know if Lisa's trying to deceive us."

"Yeah," he confirmed.

"I don't know of any way someone can conceal their true feelings from themselves," she replied. "And when I read their feelings, a part of me becomes a part of them."

"Then Lisa really wants to join us?"

"As far as I can tell," Connie said.

"And what about The Hawk?"

"What about him?"

"You weren't so happy when I showed up with him. What are his feelings?"

Connie's gaze and voice became stern. "I told you, I don't like to use that power, so I haven't. But, from what I've seen, I don't think he's a Tar, and he seems to care about you."

"I knew he was okay."

She rolled her eyes. "Yeah, you have great instincts."

"I must," Jack said. "I knew I liked you right away."

Connie looked away for a second, and then cleared her throat. "Go get some sleep."

Benny looked over the group from his spot by the entrance and watched Jack approach slowly.

"What can I do for you, Jack?" he whispered as Jack sat beside him.

Jack spoke softly. "I heard a story about Tardon and was wondering if it was true."

"The story that Tardon is so powerful because he has the power of two, and that his twin died while they were in the womb, and the twin's power was transferred to Tardon? If that's the story you're referring to, yes, I have heard that one."

"Is it true?"

"No one knows for sure," Benny replied. "Tardon is a very powerful wizard, much more powerful than most wizards, and those who fear him came up with that story to explain his power. But the truth of it is highly unlikely."

"Why?"

"Because twin births in the wizarding world are very rare," he said. "So rare that—"

"Me and Maddie are the only ones," Jack finished. "I've heard that, but there must have been others."

"None that I know of. In fact, the only time I've heard of twins was in the foretelling of your birth."

"Who made the foretelling?" Jack asked.

Benny looked down and shook his head. "You are asking questions I cannot answer. Tomorrow, you can present your questions to Stanton. Perhaps he can give you the answers you seek." He took a long look at Jack. "Though I think you may be looking for more than just answers."

Jack shrugged. "I guess maybe I am. I want to know all I can about Tardon; he must have a weakness." He paused. "And if he is so powerful, how come I was able to beat him?"

"Make no mistake, Jack. Tardon maybe the most powerful wizard ever, but when you faced him, the combination of your anger and love for you mother, along with your own great strength, exploded in a terrifying moment for Tardon. You caught him by surprise, and that's not something I expect will happen again. That's why it is so important for you and Maddie to stay together."

"I know, the power of two in one. But, if the story about Tardon is true, then he has the power of two in one, and we'll need to find a weakness to beat him."

"I see your point," Benny agreed. "But I don't have the answers you want. Hopefully, Stanton can point you towards what you're looking for."

Paths United: Chapter Three

The night passed slowly, as no one slept well. Through the tossing and turning, Maddie and Jack's eyes met several times, and without words, their sibling bond was woven tighter. Somehow, they confirmed what they needed to do, where they needed to go, and who they needed to become. They both knew they only had each other to rely on. Sure, their family was with them and would support them, but what needed to be done was something only they could accomplish. They knew it, accepted it, and even embraced it.

Finally, the night was brought to an end when Fala and two young female Gnomes entered the cave, carrying baskets containing breakfast. The two young Gnomes began unpacking the food while Fala roused the wizards, which didn't take much effort, because everyone was closer to being awake than asleep.

They sat in the familiar circle and were passing around the breakfast of breads and fruits when Maddie noticed that some people were missing. "Where are Togo and Retta?" she asked.

"Stanton has asked a service of our Chief," Fala answered. "And Retta has been encouraged to continue her assignment."

Maddie turned to Benny. "Does that mean that Retta is going to Tardon?"

"Yes," Benny replied calmly. "We must let Tardon believe that Retta has fulfilled his orders."

"But she'll be in danger!" Maddie shouted.

"Retta is well aware of that," Benny said. "But, she also knows the importance of letting Tardon believe his orders are being followed. She will be fine."

Maddie let out a slow breath. "I hope you're right."

Jack decided to jump in and change the subject. "Fala, do you know what it is that Stanton has asked Chief Togo to do?"

"My son has decided to keep that to himself, and Stanton has not been available for me to speak to."

Jack didn't know what to say. He could sense that Fala was not pleased with being kept in the dark, but how could you put someone at ease in that situation? Jack was relieved when Benny stepped in.

"Fala," Benny said. "I do know that Stanton is attending to a very important matter, and that is why he is not available to answer your questions. As for Togo not sharing what has been asked of him, I'm sure he has his reasons. But I do know that, as Chief, Togo has a responsibility to keep his people safe, and since I don't know what Stanton has asked of him, we must assume that Togo is simply fulfilling his duties."

Fala lowered her head. "That is probably the case," she agreed. "And it is not my place to question our Chief, but as a mother, I cannot help but be worried."

"I understand that," Tina said, joining the conversation. "Being the mother of children with great responsibilities can wreak havoc on the nerves. All we can do is trust in their abilities and believe that we have done our job as mothers."

Fala took Tina's hand. "I had forgotten that I was not the only mother here."

Tina squeezed Fala's hand. "Sometimes, we forget that there are allies all around us. You can talk to me whenever you need to."

"Thank you," Fala said. "And I will always be here for you." They shared a smile.

Benny stood. "We really should be getting ready to go," he instructed. "Get yourselves together, and we'll go out to the clearing."

In a short time, everyone was ready to go. Fala led them from the cave.

Benny stood before her. "Once again, I must offer you my thanks for all you have done." He bowed.

Fala returned the bow. "We have pledged our allegiance and will always be prepared to offer what help we can."

"It is appreciated more than you know," Benny said.

The rest of the wizards came forward to offer their thanks and goodbyes to Fala. Then, they formed a circle in the center of the clearing, joined hands, and vanished.

Paths United: Chapter Four

The wizards appeared on a deserted coastline, and when the sound of waves crashing on the shore and the smell of sea air met them, both Jack and Maddie were brought back to fun-filled days at the beach with their parents. But that seemed so long ago now. No one and nothing was on the beach.

Maddie turned to her mother and said, "I thought we were going to Stanton's."

"We are," she answered.

Benny gestured for everyone to follow him as he walked toward a series of large sand dunes that were topped with thick sea grass. He stopped before the largest dune, whispered something, and raised a hand. Out of the dune rose a large building that looked like a luxury beachfront home. It was dark gray with white trim, a large white porch, and big circular windows. Stanton walked out of the ornate wooden front door and stood on the porch, watching the wizards climb the stairs toward him.

"Come," he called. "The guard has already assembled in the courtyard."

Stanton led the way through the door and into the house. They walked down a long, wood paneled corridor to another door at the back of the house that opened onto an enormous courtyard filled with hundreds of people wearing hooded white cloaks.

Maddie and Jack stopped and stared at the large crowd while the others continued to follow Stanton. It was Connie who turned back and saw that the twins weren't moving. She went back to them. "Are you two coming?" she asked.

"What is all this?" Maddie asked.

"Stanton told you he was going to assemble the guard," Connie answered. "Did you think there was only a few of us? They're all waiting to hear the new strategy for our fight against Tardon."

"I would have thought Stanton would have told them," Maddie said.

Connie shook her head. "Oh, no. I'm sure he's leaving that up to *The Destined Ones*."

Maddie took a step back and looked at Jack. "You're going to have to do it. I can't speak in front of all those people."

"Oh, yes, you can," Jack said. "It was your idea; now, come on." He put an arm around Maddie's shoulder and gently steered her toward the front of the assembly where Stanton and everyone else were waiting.

They caught up with the others just as Stanton stepped before the crowd. Tina met them. "Nice of you to join us," she said. Jack and Maddie smiled their reply as Stanton began to speak.

"Members of the guard, thank you for coming—and on such short notice. Today, I bring you good news in our long battle. First, our mission to reunite *The Destined Ones* has been successful." There was a roar from the crowd and an applause that shook the ground.

Stanton held his hands high above his head, and there was immediate silence. He continued. "We have also had success in that two key members of the Tars have seen the lies that Tardon spews and left his ranks to join us. That has led us to come up with a new angle in our fight against Tardon." He glanced at Jack and Maddie. "And I will allow *The Destined Ones* to give you the details."

The crowd exploded in cheers again as Stanton gestured towards Jack and Maddie. The twins looked at each other and took a reluctant step forward. Jack leaned close to Maddie. "It's all yours, sis."

Maddie nodded and cleared her throat. "Thanks for the support, Jack." She stood silent for a moment as she took in the large crowd and felt the weight of their collective gaze bear down upon her. Her body began to tremble slightly. .

"Hello, everyone," she began, and was surprised that her voice carried loud and clear. "My name is Maddie, and my brother Jack and I are here to help you fight Tardon." She jumped as the crowd erupted in another loud applause.

Maddie looked at Jack, and he urged her to continue. Then she cleared her throat again, and the crowd quieted. "We have had two people join us who were once against us," she continued. "We think there are others who might want to change sides, but they might be too afraid. We ask that all of you who have family and friends on the wrong side to go to them and tell them about Tardon's lies. They might not be happy to see you, so be ready for that, but this is very important. If we can take some of Tardon's followers, our fight will be easier."

There was silence among the crowd as everyone began to look at one another and shake their heads. Stanton stepped forward, but Maddie's confidence had grown.

"No," she said. "I can take care of this. I realize we are asking a lot." Her voice was louder. "But, if Tardon wins, he will demand more than this from you. If we want to win, we must take from Tardon that which makes him strong: his followers. Show them Tardon is wrong, and he will be defeated. Do this and we will win."

There was another loud cheer, and Stanton smiled at Maddie before turning to the crowd. He held up his hands to quiet them. "Go," he commanded. "Bring us recruits from Tardon's own followers. Weaken him."

Stanton turned away from the crowd and addressed the group standing with him. "Come with me." He led them through the crowd, in the back door of the beach house, down a long hallway, and into a large room. Once everyone had entered the room, Stanton closed the large wooden doors.

"Please, everyone sit," Stanton said as he settled into a large leather arm chair in a corner of the room.

Everyone except Benny and Gavin, found a seat in the crowded room.

"That was very well done, Maddie," Stanton complimented. "I believe you have inspired the troops."

Ray and Tina smiled at Maddie as she looked down, and Jack patted her on the back. "Good job, sis."

"Yes," Benny agreed. "Good job, indeed."

Maddie wanted to take the focus off of herself. "So, what do we do while everyone else is recruiting?"

"We will put the rest of our plan into action," Stanton said. "I have asked Retta to continue to allow Tardon to believe that she has joined him and, since we are seeking converts, I have asked Togo to use his skills of communication with the animals to persuade the more formidable of them to come to our aid."

"Why didn't Togo tell Fala that?" Jack asked. "She seemed a bit angry that he didn't tell her what he was doing."

"Togo chose not to tell his mother so that she would not insist on going with him," Stanton said. Then he looked at Lisa. "For the time being, we will hide you and Erin. I don't want Tardon to find you, and we must make it appear that Retta has carried out her mission."

Erin leaned forward and began to protest, but Lisa put a hand on her leg and she quieted. "That's fine," Lisa said.

Stanton nodded his reply as he stood. "With that set, I think it's time for some lunch."

They walked through the house to the back deck, and feasted on a lunch more in line with what Jack and Maddie were used to: sliced turkey sandwiches, potato chips, and cookies for dessert. The deck looked out to the beach, and the sea air and rolling waves had a tranquil effect on Jack. After lunch, he walked onto the dunes and found a seat on the largest one and looked out at the waves. It didn't take long before Maddie joined him.

"Hey," she said as she reached the top of the dune and sat next to him. "What are you doing up here?"

"You have to ask?" he replied.

Maddie chuckled. "You were waiting for me to find you."

"I knew you would eventually."

"Okay," she said. "You obviously wanted to be away from everyone. What's up?"

"Well," he began. "If we're the ones who have to defeat Tardon, then I think we should know as much about him as possible."

"That makes sense," she agreed.

"The Hawk told me a story about Tardon, and I asked Benny about it, but he told me to talk to Stanton. Before I do that, though, I wanted to tell you the story."

"Okay," Maddie said. "What's the story?"

Jack recounted the tale about Tardon's twin dying in the womb and his powers being transferred to Tardon, which was what had given him his great power.

Maddie listened, and as she did, her mouth fell open. When Jack finished, she said nothing. She simply kept shaking her head until he broke the silence.

"We need to ask Stanton about this. Even if Tardon is the most powerful wizard ever, he must have a weakness. Even Superman had kryptonite."

Maddie looked at Jack, her eyes still wide. "Do you think Stanton knows his weakness?"

He shrugged. "I don't know. But, I think if he did, he would have beaten Tardon by now. Maybe he has some ideas."

Maddie stood. "We're not going to find out anything sitting here all day. Let's find Stanton and get some answers."

The twins went back to the deck and found Stanton sitting in a rocking chair, looking out to the ocean. He was alone.

Maddie looked around. "Where is everyone?"

"They've been shown to their rooms," Stanton answered. "I've been waiting for you two. Benny tells me you have some questions."

The twins took a seat in the two deck chairs that were on either side of Stanton. "Should we assume that you know what we wanted to talk to you about?" Jack asked.

Stanton smiled. "It would be safe to do, so, yes."

"So, is the story about Tardon true?" Maddie questioned.

"That's a complicated question. Tardon is very powerful, and the origin of his power is something I've tried hard to find. I believe the story of Tardon being a twin is most likely true, but whether that twin died before birth, I'm not so sure. However, Tardon's nature is something I am familiar with, and I suspect he *did* obtain his twin's power, but in a much more sinister way."

"Are you saying that Tardon stole the power from his twin?!" Jack exclaimed.

"That is what I suspect."

"He killed his own twin," Maddie gasped. "That's horrible."

"Yes," Stanton said. "It would be, but I don't believe that to be the case. I believe that Tardon has stolen his twin's powers and has been keeping his twin in captivity."

Jack scratched his head. "Not to sound like a nut job, or anything . . . but, wouldn't it be easier for Tardon to just have killed his twin?"

Stanton smirked. "That would be what, a nut job, as you say, would do. But Tardon is no ordinary nut job. He is very intelligent and calculating, and if we assume that his twin is a brother who is also identical, wouldn't it make sense to have a ready-made double should things not work out as planned and a hasty disappearance is necessary?"

"I could see that," Maddie said. "But how do we find out if all of this is true?"

Stanton got up and walked to the railing of the deck. He took in a long breath of sea air and then turned to face the twins. "It is an ancient and complicated spell that is needed to transfer the powers of one wizard to another, and there is only one wizard I know of who could perform such magic. The Spell Master."

"The Spell Master?" Jack asked, scratching his head. "Can't all wizards perform spells?"

"Unfortunately, no," Stanton said. "Most magic does not require a spell or an incantation to manifest itself—only a desire by the wizard. However, spells were used in ancient times to perform very dark and dangerous magic. There were only a few wizards who could cast a successful spell, and now, there is only one: the Spell Master."

"So," Maddie said. "If we can find this Spell Master, he can tell us the secret of Tardon's power."

"Much easier said than done," Stanton pointed out. "The Spell Master has not been seen in many years, and no one seems to know where he has gone." He paused. "I have looked. But, it seems to me that someone who may know the secret of Tardon's power could also be a danger to him . . ."

"Do you think Tardon killed him?" Maddie asked.

"I doubt it. The Spell Master could be very valuable to Tardon, it's more likely—"

"That he has him locked away," Jack finished.

"But where?" Maddie added.

"Yes," Stanton said. "*That* is the question."

Paths United: Chapter Five

Jack spent the rest of the afternoon away from everyone. He walked along the beach, rocked in one of the rocking chairs on the deck, and eventually, made his way to a small bedroom reserved for him. The room wasn't much. It had bleached wooden floors, wooden planked walls that matched the floor, a small bed tucked into a corner, and a desk with one chair along the wall opposite the bed.

Jack lay back on the bed, his arms folded behind his head, staring at the ceiling while over and over in his head he replayed the conversation he and Maddie had had with Stanton. Was Stanton right? Was Tardon holding his twin in captivity? Had he really stolen his twin's powers? Before he and Maddie faced Tardon, they needed to know the truth. *But where to begin?*

A knock on the door startled him out of his thoughts, and he sat up on the edge of the bed. "Come in," he called.

The door opened and The Hawk stepped in, closing it behind him. He pulled the small chair away from the desk and placed it in front of Jack, taking a seat. "How you doing, kid?"

"I'm okay," Jack said. "I'm just doing some thinking."

"I've noticed. I hope you know that I'll do anything I can to help you."

Jack nodded. "I know, and thanks."

"Don't thank me too soon. I want to help you, and I will." The Hawk looked down. "But, there's something I have to do first."

"What is it?"

"You and Maddie have asked everyone to go their families and try to bring them to our side. I think it's time I go to mine."

Jack stood. "But your family wants you dead!"

"Not all of them. I think if I get my brother alone, he'll listen to me."

"You came back here because of me. I'm going with you."

"I came back here because it was the right thing to do," The Hawk corrected. "You don't need to come with me."

"But I think I should."

The Hawk shook his head. "You're not going to put yourself in danger for me."

"You know what me and Maddie are here to do, right? I don't think a little more danger will matter one way or another."

Standing, The Hawk said, "I appreciate that you want to come with me, but I think this is something I have to do on my own."

Jack could see there was no budging his friend on the issue. "Okay, but I expect to see you soon."

"You will," The Hawk assured him. When he opened the door to leave the room, Maddie was standing there, just about to knock.

"Sorry," The Hawk said, stepping around Maddie and walking down the hall.

Maddie watched The Hawk walk away. "Is everything okay?" she asked her brother.

"He's leaving," Jack informed her. "He wants to try to convince his family to join our side."

Maddie scratched her head as she sat in the chair. "Don't they want to kill him?"

He nodded. "Yeah, but he thinks he can get to them through his brother."

"I hope he's right."

"Me too," Jack said.

"I've been thinking about what Stanton told us."

Jack sat on the edge of the bed. "So have I."

"Do you think he's right?" she asked.

"I do. But what do we do about it?"

"If we work on the theory that Stanton's right, then the Spell Master is the one who made Tardon so powerful and—"

"He can take the power away," Jack finished for her.

"Yes," Maddie said. "So, I think our first move is to find the Spell Master."

"How are we going to do that? Even Stanton doesn't know where to look."

"I've been thinking about that, too," she said. "And I think I know where to begin, but we have to do this on our own."

End . . .

ABOUT THE AUTHOR

Cris Pasqueralle is the author of the bestselling Destiny Revealed, book one of The Destiny trilogy. He is a retired NYC Police officer who lives on Long Island, NY with his wife and two daughters. He is very passionate about fostering a love of reading in young people and believes that reading is the gateway to success.

Follow Cris @:
Facebook: www.facebook.com/authorcrispasqueralle
Twitter: http://twitter.com/cpasqueralle
Instagram: https://instagram.com/cpasqueralle
Tumblr: http://authorcris.tumblr.com

MORE BOOKS FROM THE DESTINY TRILOGY

DESTINY REVEALED: BOOK 1

QUEST FOR DESTINY: BOOK 3

Cosby Media Productions™

Entertaining the Mind, and Inspiring the Soul

www.cosbymediaproductions.com

www.ingramcontent.com/pod-product-compliance
Lightning Source LLC
Chambersburg PA
CBHW070552180626
46817CB00005B/1803

* 9 7 8 0 6 9 2 5 8 2 1 0 7 *